CRIMSON PROMISE

A Vampire Romance

L.T. Whitney

QUILL & SCRIBE
PUBLISHING

Printed in the United States of America.

For more information, or to book an event, contact:

ltwhitneyauthor@gmail.com

Book design by L.T. Whitney

Cover design by L.T. Whitney

Title text design by Julie Schorr

ISBN - Paperback: 979-8-9897215-0-4

ISBN - E-book : 979-8-9897215-1-1

First Edition: June 2024, Quill & Scribe Publishing

For those who believe in love.

No matter what form it comes in.

PLAYLIST

Look What You Made Me Do
{Taylor Swift}

Haunted (Taylor's Version)
{Taylor Swift}

I Put A Spell On You
{Annie Lennox}

Bad Things {Jace Everett}

Bones {Little Big Town}

Man or a Monster
{Sam Tinnesz, Zayde Wolf}

I See Red
{Everybody Loves an Outlaw}

The Lion The Beast The Beat
{Grace Potter & The
Nocturnals}

Hot Summer Night
{Grace Potter & The
Nocturnals}

Arcade {Duncan Laurence}

Way down We Go {KALEO}

Running Up That Hill (Violin)
{Joel Sunny}

Game of Survival {Ruelle}

Rival {Ruelle}

Monsters {Ruelle}

Everybody Wants To Rule The
World {Lorde}

Don't Blame Me {Taylor Swift}

This Is How Villains Are
Made {Ruben K, Alexa Ray}

Morally Grey {April Jai}

Who's Afraid Of Little Old
Me? {Taylor Swift}

AUTHOR'S NOTE:

This novel is an adult work of fiction featuring adult language and situations. The following work may contain content related to non-consensual sex, rape, vampires, blood, weapon violence, death, suicide, sex, verbal/emotional abuse, and physical abuse. While I have done my best to include all triggering situations, please note this is not an all-inclusive list. If any of these topics are triggering, please take care while reading.

CRIMSON

PROMISE

PROLOGUE

ALARIC

1873

Panic rose in my body as the distinctive, metallic aroma filled the air. Gruesome pools of rust-colored blood encompassed me. Wooden beams of the cottage ceiling came into view as my vision focused on the sight in front of me. *Rosie, no, not my Rosie.* I sat up, taking in my surroundings, horror blooming within me with each passing moment.

My fiancé lay in a crumpled heap on the floor of her cottage. Crimson streaks stained her emerald dress, and her scarlet hair splayed across her face in ringlets. Dried blood and fang marks covered her throat. There was only one explanation for how this happened. I did this. I killed my Rosie, the love of my life. *Gods, what had I done?*

1

COSETTE

Present Day

"Come on, Cosette. Come out with us!" My friend Libby whined. She had begged me all week to go to a club with her and a group of our friends, despite me telling her multiple times that I had no interest in going. Clubs weren't my thing; give me a steaming cup of tea, a book, and a cozy blanket instead.

Libby and I both worked at the university library, and I loved it. Libby, not so much. I couldn't imagine a more perfect job for a bookish literature major like me. I mean, come on, my name is Cosette. Clearly, my parents named me after their favorite book.

I loathed the idea of clubbing, but Libby wouldn't stop begging until I agreed. Plus, she was one of my closest friends. This time, I'd have to take one for the team.

"Fine," I relinquished, "but only for an hour. I have to work tomorrow."

Libby jumped for joy. She began texting away on her cell, gathering the troops. I busied myself with the list of reserve materials I needed to pull for the next round of students coming in.

I glanced at the reserve slip in my hand; a request for historical medieval texts found in our rare collections room. Getting from the circulation desk to the room took a bit of a walk, but one I welcomed if it meant I was in the presence of such exquisite documents and texts. I made my way to the east staircase and headed down to the serenely quiet room. Being there soothed my mind, and the scent was intoxicating. I got to work finding the books on my list straight away.

While not old itself, the rare collections section housed the library's most ancient and treasured texts. It was the one room in our building that lacked the sterile library feel, and instead held a lovely, earthy aroma and invited any who came there to rediscover the past. A set of ornate bookshelves spanned the far wall and displayed the oldest books, many with unique leather covers.

Halfway through my list, a peculiar sensation prickled my neck. Goosebumps rose on my skin. *Was someone watching me?* I whipped my head around, expecting a patron, who needed something from me to be standing in the doorway, only to find an empty hallway.

I went back to my work. After I pulled all the materials, I glanced at the time and realized I was running late. I made quick work of boxing up all the texts and was taking them to the reserve desk when the same prickly sensation skittered down my spine. My breath hitched, and I froze, terrified to turn around. I focused my hearing toward the darkened, empty hallway, straining to listen for footsteps or other telltale noises. Nothing but silence echoed in my ears. Gathering my courage, I turned around and braced myself, holding the tension in my body. A breath of surprise escaped my mouth. The hallway remained empty.

Without a doubt, I needed more sleep. I wouldn't rest tonight, though, with my promise to go clubbing. With a sigh, I headed to the loan counter. I dropped off my box of reserve materials I had gathered and grabbed my belongings before leaving for the day.

A perk of working at a university library was the surplus of student housing in the area. While I wasn't a student any longer, I wasn't a grandma either. Being around the younger crowd didn't bother me, plus I found a cheap deal for an apartment; the quick commute to work didn't hurt either. I considered myself lucky to have found a quiet apartment block that offered serenity over parties.

I hurried to my apartment, made a cup of tea, and hopped in the shower. Taking a whiff of my citrus body wash, I wondered if Libby would let me leave the club after an hour. She would, in all likelihood, whine and ask me to stay. I'd have to set a strong boundary with her, which hasn't been my strong suit in the past.

Once out of the shower and wrapped in a towel, I stared into my closet. Ugh. I owned nothing that screamed club chic. I was more of a jeans and sweater kind of gal. What did a twenty-six-year-old wear to a club that didn't scream designated driver, chaperone, or you're-too-old-to-be-here?

I shoved some hangers aside and reached into the far corner, removing a relic from my college days: a black, strapless, body-hugging dress. Pulling it on, it just covered my ass. Needless to say, my butt had ballooned since I wore it last. Still, it was all I had, so I completed my outfit with a pair of sleek, patent leather stiletto heels, and draped a long silver chain around my neck.

I added a touch of red lipstick to my natural makeup and curled my hair in waves, allowing them to graze my shoulder blades. I grabbed my clutch as someone knocked on my door. It must be Libby. She was always punctual when it came to going clubbing. Any other time, not so much.

"Wow, Cosette, you look hot! Where on earth did you find your dress?" Libby stood in my living room wearing a skin-tight lime green dress that barely covered, well, anything.

"Oh, it's a fossil from my college days," I said, rolling my eyes.

"I think you look amazing." Libby glanced at her watch. "We better go or we'll have to wait in line."

"We wouldn't want that, would we?" I snarked.

"Hush. Come on." Libby grabbed my wrist, practically dragging me from the apartment.

It didn't take long for me to regret my choice of footwear, solidifying my opinion that I was, in fact, too old to be doing this. My pumps pinched my swollen feet and caused them to sweat. I was thankful we made it to the club without my feet bleeding. We lined up in the queue, staring at a giant, burly and tattooed bouncer. Libby flirted with him, and with a brief wait, we entered Club Dynamo.

Inside was loud and chaotic as the bass reverberated through my body. I stood in the sea of patrons who gyrated amidst the flashing lights and smoky air. All the stimulation assaulted my senses, causing me to desperately want to go home. But Libby and our friends would never let that happen. I'd promised her an hour and would at least give her an hour. I could endure this place for a measly sixty minutes.

I headed to the bar to grab a beverage. "White Zinfandel, please," I told the bartender. I'm not a huge drinker but enjoy a glass of wine from time to time.

"Sure thing." He smiled at my request. My order didn't align with the younger crowd here who preferred shots or beer.

He set the wineglass in front of me with a polite grin. I paid and then sipped, turning to face the dance floor. I watched as Libby and our friends danced like maniacs, grinding up on one another. I let out a laugh, then detected eyes on me from my peripheral vision. A man—somewhat older than me—sat beside me, his muddy work boots propped up on the bar stool underneath him. His torn and stained boot-cut jeans had seen better days. He wore a grungy gray t-shirt paired with a flannel button-down. His hair, full of stringy, oily wisps, hung in his eyes.

"Friends of yours?" he asked, nodding toward the dance floor.

I smirked. "Guilty as charged."

"How come you're not out there with them?" He took a sip of his Bud Light.

"This isn't my kind of scene. I only came because my friend forced me to."

He leaned closer and shouted to me above the music, "What *is* your scene?" His breath had the scent of decay combined with the aroma of beer and strong body odor. A sinking feeling in my stomach made me want to move away.

"Not here," I shouted. This guy was barking up the wrong tree. I wasn't looking for a hookup, but I was looking for a way out of that awkward situation. "Do you know where the restroom is?"

"Sure. Let me show you. I've got to take a piss myself."

I didn't want to be rude and figured I'd hide in the bathroom for a while, then meet up with Libby and go home.

We both rose from our stools and he pointed toward the direction he wanted me to go. Mr. Bud Light led me through the club, snaking through the outskirts of the dance floor, toward the back of the club, and to a door I assumed led to the bathrooms.

I opened the door to step into the hallway outside the bathrooms, with Mr. Bud Light following right behind me. I glanced back at him and said, "Where's the..."

Before I got my words out, Mr. Bud Light, with a heavy hand, guided me out the door, closing it behind him. We were in a dark alley with an overflowing dumpster and the smell of rotting garbage. No security or street lights. The only source of light was a single light above the door.

I froze for a moment, attempting to digest my confusion and then my stomach dropped. "This isn't the restroom."

Mr. Bud Light remained silent. Panic swirled inside me. My breathing turned shallow and my heart pounded as if it would beat out of my chest. I needed to call for help or run, but my feet seemed glued to the spot. And then I felt his breath on my neck. His exhale unfurled into my nostrils, leading me to gag at the repugnant smell.

His hand touched my hair and whispered, "It's only us here. Now we can get to know one another."

His words sent a shiver up my spine. My body shook from the coursing adrenaline while my stomach was doing flips. I couldn't move past my brain telling me to be cordial in my exit.

"I need to go back inside to find my friends, or they'll worry," I squeaked.

"Who needs 'em? It's me, you, and your sexy ass dress," he said, looking me up and down.

Before I responded, he ran his hands along the sides of my waist and down over my hips, rubbing my ass, and slipping his fingers under the hem of my dress. His hands drifted along my body with one hand upward under my chin, tilting my head back, while the other went to my lips. I screamed and shoved his hands away.

He grabbed my arms as I struggled out of his grip. I was pushed against a hard surface, my head radiating with pain from the impact. I gasped for air while hands were pinned around my neck. No one could hear me. Not a single person knew where I was. No one could save me from him.

2

COSETTE

Present Day

Digging my fingers into my attacker's grip, I gasped for air, my vision growing fuzzy. My consciousness seeped from me, dimming into a dark abyss as if I had closed my eyes. And then the pressure around my neck loosened. I inhaled. My thoughts jumbled together as I tried to think and slow my breathing. *Is this really happening? Come on, Cosette, protect yourself. Why is this guy attacking me? Someone, anyone, please help me!*

The coldness of the brick building behind my back leaked through my clothes. Attempting to pull myself out of my thoughts, I focused on my breathing, counting to myself. *One, two, three, in, one, two, three, out.*

I opened my eyes, glancing around for my attacker, only to discern a shadowy figure looming at the edge of the darkness of the alleyway. My heartbeat drummed in my chest as alarm gripped me. With a breath caught in my throat, the icy grip of worry seized my thoughts of the ominous figure before me. I shoved my attacker, hoping to put distance between myself and the strangers in the alley but to little avail.

"Unhand her!" The shadow stepped forward into the single light above the club's back door, revealing his strong jaw and flared nostrils. He was within arm's distance, using his stature to loom over my assailant.

"Fuck off, dude! We're having a moment here," my attacker yelled, irritation in his voice.

"Get off me!" I screamed, moving my body and trying to jerk out of his grip.

"I think the lady made it quite clear. Unhand her before I do it for you," the shadow threatened, stepping closer. I peered at my rescuer, drawn to his piercing blue eyes and dark brown hair falling in disheveled waves. He was taller than my attacker and with a muscular build. His jeans and t-shirt clung to him without being too tight.

"We're fine, man. Get your own chick. This one's occupied."

Mr. Bud Light couldn't take the hint. He continued to grip my dress, pulling me closer to him. He snickered before saying, "Come closer, little bird." His mouth turned upward into an unsettling Cheshire grin. My body shook from the adrenaline coursing through my body, leaving me nauseous.

"I said, unhand *mon tresor!*" The shadow stormed the distance between us, grabbed my attacker by the back of his shirt, and separated us. The figure slung my attacker out toward the alley before grabbing hold of him again and hurling him into the wall.

As my attacker screamed in pain, I stood near the back door, frightened and mesmerized by the display in front of me. Before I processed what was happening, the mystery man placed his hands on both sides of my attacker's head and twisted. The audible crunch was enough to make me vomit.

"Is…Is he dead?" My voice trembled as bile burned my throat.

My rescuer strolled in my direction. "Are you alright, miss?" He said with a small lilt of a French accent in his voice.

I gulped. My body was cold and heavy, and my head spun. I couldn't answer my rescuer as I gazed into his concerned eyes. "I don't know, I think so," I murmured, wiping the vomit from my mouth. Instinctively, I took a step back as he approached me, unsure of my rescuer's true intentions.

"He didn't hurt you, did he? Defile you?" He focused on me with his searing blue eyes. Intense and clear, like a sapphire that seemed to penetrate one's soul. But, *defile me? Who says something like that?*

"No, things didn't get far. I didn't know him. He was supposed to be showing me where the restroom was," I choked out between sobs.

"It's okay. You've been through something traumatizing." He paused, taking a step toward me. We stood in the silence for a beat as he wiped his hands on his pants nervously while my sobs quieted. He cleared his throat before continuing, "I'm glad it didn't get far before I intervened. My name's Alaric. Why don't you allow me to escort you to safety? Or do you want me to call the police? I could walk you to the station if you want to go in person."

"No, no. I don't want to involve the police. He only roughed me up a bit. Plus, I've been drinking, so I'm sure they'll say it's my fault. I want to go home."

His expression softened and his shoulders relaxed. "It's not your fault. Though I understand why you don't want to deal with the police. Will you at least let me escort you home?"

I took a step back and thought for a moment about how to proceed while reaching into my clutch for my cell phone. Every part of my mind screamed for me to run away in fear, I was exhausted. Alaric seemed likable and while I wasn't keen on him knowing where I lived, I wasn't thrilled to walk home alone, either. All I wanted was to leave this alley and arrive safely to my apartment, even if that meant him coming with me. I glanced at my phone.

Libby: Where are you, Cosette?

Libby: Did you already leave?

Libby: We're headed to Sunshine Bar.

Join us if you want.

Thanks for your concern, Lib.

I sighed. "Well, I guess I'm heading home. My friends have already left."

"I'll escort you home. You shouldn't walk alone," Alaric said.

"Okay, let me send my friend Libby a text first."

Cosette: I'm heading home now.

I'll text you when I am home.

If you don't receive a text from me, call the cops.

I'll explain later.

With my text sent, I stowed my phone in my purse and pointed toward my complex. "That way."

We walked down the street toward my apartment in silence. The quiet wasn't awkward; rather, it soothed me after the loud club and the scuffle in the alley. I reflected on how Alaric rescued me and asked, "You called me something when you pulled the guy off me. It wasn't English. What did you call me?"

"*Mon tresor.*"

I tilted my head and stared up at him.

"It's French. It means 'my treasure.'"

"Your treasure? How can I be your treasure when you don't know my name?"

He gave me a thoughtful smile. This guy was a little weird, but I wouldn't have to put up with him for long. I longed to crawl into bed and pretend to forget this whole evening once I got home.

We stopped at the gate to my complex, resembling two people wrapping up a first date. Awkward.

Alaric gestured to my building. "Your castle awaits, my lady."

"Thank you for the escort."

"Anytime, *mon tresor.*" He bowed his head.

"My name's Cosette, by the way. Goodnight, Alaric," I said, opening the wrought-iron gate and stepping through.

"Goodnight, Cosette." Alaric tipped his head toward me, as I crossed the darkened courtyard and ascended the stairs to my door. As I closed my door, I saw him turn and continue down the street past my complex while I thought about the terrifying turn my night had taken.

3

ALARIC

1873

I was made a vampire when I was 28 years old. It happened so quickly that I didn't even fight. One minute, I was walking to the tavern to enjoy a round of ale with my mates, and then suddenly, a tall shadow dragged me into a back alley. I felt the life drain out of me as the shadow fed from me. As I approached the precipice of death, a warm, tingling sensation coursed throughout my body, and the seemingly inescapable hands of death disappeared. I felt invincible.

I glanced around, attempting to find the shadow that had attacked me, but all I could see was the darkened alleyway behind the tavern. As quickly as the shadow had appeared, it had vanished, leaving me to ponder what had happened. Any attempt to recall the details left me with an onslaught of headache-inducing thoughts. No longer in the mood to socialize or explain my disheveled appearance, I began the walk back to my flat.

I couldn't quite wrap my mind around what had just occurred, and as I neared my home, a gnawing, hunger-like sensation grew in the pit of my stomach. *What was happening to me? What happened in that alleyway?*

The events I could recall came in flashes. It was as if my mind was preventing me from fully remembering. A quick moving shadow. The press of teeth on my neck. Everything after that was lost to the darkness. I awoke in the alley with nothing more than my fractured memory and aching body.

My thoughts were distracting me. Attempting to make sense of what happened to me, I wandered the streets of the village and found myself at Rosie's door. The cottage was a quaint abode on the outskirts of the village, nestled against the edge of the forest. As I had the cottage in my sight, the wooden building made of natural and neutral colors, I noticed how it blended into the forest and had a small trickle of smoke of a dimming fire coming from the chimney. It wasn't typical for a young lady Rosie's age to be living alone or have their own cottage. She had inherited it after the death of her parents as she was their only child and I was thankful she had no roommates or family living with her.

I knocked on her door. "Rosie, it's me," I announced. "It's Alaric."

A few moments later, I heard trudging coming from inside. She opened the door slowly, leaving only enough room for her face to peer out. She groggily gazed up at me before a look of shock graced her face, and she swung the door open in reaction to my bedraggled appearance.

"Alaric! What in heaven's name are you doing here? What happened? Are you alright?" she exclaimed, her brows creased with worry.

"Do not worry, *mon tresor*. I'm alright," I said. "I had a bit of a tousle en route to the tavern."

"Oh, my goodness. Are you injured?" She asked, looking my body over.

"No, my love. I'm just tired," I exhaled.

"Well, come in, come in," she waved me into her cozy cottage.

I was thankful for the warmth from the fire and Rosie's embrace. I was still trying to collect my thoughts and feelings from earlier in the evening. Desire to tell her about what had happened enveloped me, but my memories were too faint to articulate.

I couldn't ignore what seemed to be a newfound ability to smell even the most minute crumb. As I walked past Rosie, I could smell the rose petals of her perfume and her freshly-bathed skin. The hints of citrus mingled with the rose petals, creating a unique smell I hadn't noticed before.

Smells were not the only thing that seemed to catch my attention, but minor details as well. Sounds were louder, the once subtle cracks and pops of the fire flared in my ears while the colors of the flames became more vibrant. The flooring of the cottage seemed deeper in color and the wood grain of the ceiling beams painted designs in my vision while all my senses formed a mysterious feeling within me that was becoming almost impossible to ignore. I found myself drawn to the thrumming vessel in Rosie's neck, watching its rhythmic, steady beat. I had never noticed this before. When she caught me staring at her neck, I glanced away.

"Are you alright, darling?" she asked.

"I'm…I'm not sure," I admitted. "I don't feel like myself."

"How so, dear?" Rosie stepped forward, her eyes scrutinizing my appearance. As she moved closer, I could inhale her scent and feel the heat of her skin, near enough for her to kiss me. She craned her head, examining my neck.

A moment of realization crossed her face, her eyes widened. "Alaric, someone has fed from you!" Her face was aghast with horror. She paused for a long moment. "I think you're a vampire now," she said worriedly.

"A what?"

"The...the fang marks on your neck. When a vampire feeds on you until you're on the brink of death, you become one of them," Rosie said.

I could hardly believe what Rosie was telling me. *Vampires didn't exist, did they?* I didn't feel that different. I recalled little from the physical altercation I had had earlier in the evening. I simply thought I had been roughed up a bit.

"Rosie," I breathed, looking deeply into her eyes. Now I began to really think about what Rosie had said. It would explain why I felt out of sorts.

"Alaric," she said, looking my face over. "Let me help you."

I remained silent but nodded. Rosie busied herself with putting a pot of water on to boil. She went to her sewing basket to remove small pieces of cotton cloth and nosed around on a nearby shelf for a tonic or tincture before pouring a small amount into a bowl. As the pressure behind my eyes increased and my wounds throbbed, she dipped the cloth into the steaming water before dabbing lightly.

"Sorry, love," she said as I winced.

"Don't be. I appreciate the care you give me." I smiled, looking up at her delicate face.

"Of course."

She continued to cleanse my wounds until the water took on a pink tinge, and the rag was stained with my blood. Rosie cleared her throat as if she was preparing to say something to me. After drying my face, Rosie stepped into her bedroom, returning a moment later with an object in her hand.

"I want you to have this," she said, placing a necklace in my hand. I looked down to see a golden chain with a ruby-red amulet attached. She must have seen my confusion, prompting her to say, "The village will be dangerous for you now. If anyone finds out, the town will burn you."

Gesturing to the necklace, she continued, "This amulet has been passed down through my family. It is powerful. As long as you wear it, no one will know you are a vampire and cannot kill you."

"Thank you," I said with gratitude in my voice. I glanced down at the necklace, my eyebrows drawn. She looked down at me, reading the concern on my face.

"You're safe with me, my love." She smiled and leaned down to kiss me.

I inclined my head, deepening the kiss, and placed my hands on her hips, drawing her closer to me. She embraced me, drawing in my affection like she needed it to breathe. I was so thankful for Rosie. She meant the world to me, and her acceptance of the thing I had become meant more than any protection the amulet could offer me.

I ended our kiss to ask, "Where did you get the amulet?"

"My father gave it to me before he died. For centuries, my family has had an alliance with vampire kind. In return for our help, the local vampires protect my family from outside vampires and other threats. A vampire gave my father the amulet after he saved the vampire's life." Rosie explained.

I flipped the amulet over in my hand, examining its intricacies before attempting to place it back in her hands. "Rosie, I cannot allow you to give up protection for yourself and your family for me," I said.

Her eyes as well as her words pleaded with me. "Alaric, I cannot let you go unprotected, for you will surely perish if you do not wear the amulet. Please, it is the only way for us to be together," Rosie insisted.

She frantically gripped my arms in her attempt to convince me to accept the charm. I relinquished to her insistence. Hooking my fingers around the golden chain, I placed the necklace over my head and underneath my shirt. Rosie smiled at the act and stepped closer to me, placing her arms around my neck. She gazed up at me as I moved my arms to encircle her.

Rosie and I had not been together intimately as we were waiting for our marital bed. However, the recent events seemed to have made us both reconsider. We remained in our close embrace, gazing into each other's eyes for quite some time.

Breaking eye contact, I leaned down, slowly caressing her face and brushing a stray ringlet of red hair out of her face. Rosie tipped her chin up toward me, staring at me with her soulful eyes. She let out a sound that closely resembled a mouse squeak as I placed my lips on top of hers. I took my time, practically inhaling her, her scent, her essence. Gods, she smelled amazing. I just couldn't get enough of her. I couldn't get close enough to her. Her presence made me feel a mixture of anticipation and an unquenchable need.

"Rosie, I need you," I murmured into her hair.

"I need you too, Alaric. Each moment that passes makes me want you more." She gripped my shirt, drawing me closer to her.

"I know we had agreed to wait...," I trailed off as I ran my hands down the soft curves of her body.

"I know. We did, but that feels unimportant now. I don't want us to wait any longer. I love you, and forgive me for being so forthright, but I want you in my bed as well."

I had never heard her speak so openly. It was considered the gentlemanly thing to do to respect your future wife's wishes regarding intimacy. I never wanted Rosie to feel pressured to take things further than she wanted to so

I decided to let her make the first move if her opinion ever changed.

"You're sure then?" I asked.

"Yes," she replied. "I want nothing more than to be the closest I can to you. Now that you're a vampire, waiting doesn't seem to be important any longer."

She looked up toward my face, stepping up on her toes to reach my lips. Rosie searched my eyes for a moment before planting her lips on mine. I deepened the kiss, inviting her tongue into my mouth. She tasted sweet and divine. She returned in kind by opening her mouth and sucking my tongue into hers.

"Rosie," I groaned.

She was turning my arousal into a beast that I wouldn't be able to restrain for much longer. Gods help me if she decides against me in her bed. Lust and attraction coursed through my body with electrifying intensity.

A new feeling arose within me; a foreign, primal urge. Suddenly, I felt a sensation in my mouth. It wasn't entirely painful, more like discomfort mixed with hint of pleasure. As the sensation reached a precipice, I growled, feeling my canines elongate to form fangs.

Rosie drew in a breath, a slight tremor in her voice. "Father told me what vampire fangs looked like, but seeing them in person is more frightening than I expected."

I expected her to retreat from me, but she didn't move. Instead, she leaned further into me, tracing her index finger over my fangs; an oddly calming and erotic act.

"I suppose that is how you will gain sustenance now," Rosie said, pricking her finger on the tip of my fang as she inspected it.

Her expertise of vampires surprised me, however, it seemed her father didn't volunteer everything he knew about them. Unfortunately, Rosie was the only source of information on my kind, but it would have to do.

"I believe you're correct," I admitted.

Rosie thought for a moment and, after straightening her posture, offered, "Feed from me."

"Rosie, I can't do that. I don't want to hurt you. I don't even know *how* to feed from you." I could feel the panic rise in me. Rosie then craned her neck toward my mouth, allowing me better access.

The closer my mouth got to her neck, the harder it felt to resist feeding from Rosie. "Please, Alaric. Just do it. Put your lips on my neck," she begged.

I rested my lips on her neck, drinking in her smell and the taste of her skin.

"You smell delicious." My lips ran the length of her neck, trying to restrain myself from going any farther.

"I bet I'll taste delicious too. Let me be your first feed, Alaric. It will be special for both of us to give ourselves to each other." She drew me in closer and planted a kiss on my lips. I could not withstand my desire for Rosie any longer. It was as if I had become an animal.

I ripped open the neck of her nightgown, exposing her breasts. I took a step back to admire them. Her skin was the color of cream, while her nipples were the lightest shade of pink. She stared at me with wide eyes and her mouth parted slightly, expecting me to feed from her as she craned her neck back. However, there were other things I was dying to do to her first.

I approached her again, gliding my hands over her naked back and up into her ringlets. I tipped her head back and kissed her. I could never tire of this. She moaned into my mouth, which only set my arousal burning even hotter for her. I removed the rest of her nightgown and laid her down on her bed.

"Oh, Rosie. I love you. I love everything about you," I exhaled as I looked over every angle of her body, running my hands on every one of her curves. I wanted to admire her body and memorize every inch of her.

"I love you," she smiled, looking down her naked body toward me. I nestled myself in between her legs, my head lying on her abdomen.

She lay there, seemingly without a care in the world and unashamed of her body. I peppered tiny kisses down her belly and down the inside of each thigh. She mewled like a kitten at my touch. My arousal coursed throughout my body, and the twitching in my cock was getting more and more persistent. I couldn't wait to feel how warm she was or know how she tasted.

I sat up briefly and pulled my shirt over my head and down my arms. Rosie sat up and assisted me with unbuttoning my pants and unmentionables. Now that I matched Rosie's state of undress, I turned my attention to Rosie's apex.

After thoroughly attending to her inner thighs, I had Rosie squirming and giggling with desire. I ran my fingers over her mound and down her seam, feeling her arousal. She was so wet. Not wanting to hurt her, I slid one finger inside her in tiny increments, locking my eyes on her. Her face flashed a small grimace, but soon she moaned in pleasure.

Rosie's sounds spurred me on as I added another finger into her folds. I could no longer resist tasting her. I needed to devour her. I flattened my tongue, licked her seam from bottom to top, and sucked her pleasure spot into my mouth. Rosie moaned and writhed beneath me as I teased her nub. Her body began to shift as she was getting closer and closer to her climax. I wanted her right on the edge, right when she was about to spill over.

When I sensed her muscles contracting and her breath increasing, I removed my mouth from her slit and continued working her with my fingers as I readied myself into position. I hovered over her body and lined my cock up to her entrance. I continued to caress her clit while I moved myself inside her, inch by inch, allowing her body to accommodate me. At the moment I felt Rosie quake from pleasure, I thrust my entire length into her. She gasped and cried out with ecstasy.

I rocked back and forth, slamming into her again and again. She felt amazing, and thrusting my dick to the hilt was the most delicious sensation. I never wanted this feeling to end. I couldn't believe that I got to have Rosie like this for the rest of our lives. She continued to keep pace with me, matching every rocking and plunging motion.

I was approaching my own orgasm when my fangs elongated, and an intense desire to feed surged through my body. As if by magic or our current connection, Rosie moved her head to the side, inviting me to feed from her.

"I trust you, Alaric," she said.

I was hesitant. I didn't know what to expect of myself or if I would hurt Rosie. She was putting all her faith in me.

No longer able to fight my desire for Rosie or her blood, I sank my fangs into her neck. She winced and cried out at the intrusion into her skin, but her tears soon turned to heated moans of pleasure as I sucked and lapped up her blood. Knowing she wasn't in pain only fueled me to keep going and soon I was taking slow and full sucks of her blood. The taste was incredible, exotic and sweet, yet earthy and familiar.

Lost in my arousal and senses, I fed on Rosie. She didn't fight, and instead, she embraced me with her body and continued to derive her own pleasures from my sucking. I knew I needed to stop. I couldn't draw too much blood from her or I'd hurt her. She had already been so generous in giving herself to me in so many ways tonight. I had no reason to be greedy. I felt her hand touch my arm with a bit more force, seeming to summon me to stop.

I tried to pull away, but my fangs seemed to be magnetized to her neck. As I tried to remove myself from her, Rosie seemed to fight less and less. The need to satiate myself overpowered my desire to keep Rosie safe. Her limbs barely moved. She was no longer making any noise. From out of the corner of my eye, I could see her skin had turned ashen. At this realization, I extracted my fangs from Rosie's neck. I sat up and looked at her lifeless body. Calling out, "Rosie! Rosie, my love! *Mon tresor!*"

Her chest was no longer rising. I placed an ear to her chest. Nothing. Her heart no longer beat within her beautiful body. I let out a pained howl. "Rosie!" I sobbed and held her.

Rosie was dead.

4

COSETTE

Present Day

My phone alarm range at 7 A. M. I rolled over with my head pounding, regretting my choice to go out last night. Thankfully, it was Saturday, and all the college students were at home asleep. Very few came to study on a Saturday morning, unless it was dead week and finals were upon them.

I trudged to the kitchen and put the kettle on to boil. This hot cup of tea couldn't come together fast enough. With the water boiling, I poured it into my cup to steep. As I stared at the tea leaves, my thoughts wandered back to last night. The memories flooded over me, sending a shiver up my spine as I recalled my assault. My mind kept returning to Alaric. He was so mysterious. So striking. Breathtakingly beautiful. He was the epitome of tall, dark, and handsome.

I snapped myself out of my daydream long enough to scarf down my breakfast, guzzled my cup of tea, and hopped in the shower. I scurried to dress in my typical work attire: jeans, a sweater, and ballet flats. I pulled my chestnut hair into a low ponytail and grabbed my purse to head out the door.

On my walk to work, I took in the sunshine and the quiet morning. Shops were opening, foot and car traffic were minimal. I let my thoughts wander back again to Alaric. Damn, I couldn't stop thinking about him. It's not like I would ever see him again. *Get over it, Cosette!*

I opened the lobby doors of the library and began my opening duties, preparing for a slow day at work. My phone dinged as I shelved book returns with a text from Libby.

Libby: That was a crazy text I got from you last night.

Glad you made it home safely. What happened? Spill!

Cosette: Too much to text while I'm at work, but I'll fill you in later.

Don't think I'm not pissed at you for leaving me at Dynamo last night.

Libby: I'm so sorry Cosette. We tried to find you.

I thought you were fed up with being out and went home.

I had no idea you were still there.

Cosette: I'm still mad at you, Lib. I was attacked!

If it wasn't for this guy coming along, saving me,

and then making sure I got home okay, I don't know if I would be alive today.

I hadn't processed much from last night, and the more I texted with Libby, the angrier I became with her and with the situation as a whole. The more we texted, the more it became apparent that Libby wasn't grasping the seriousness of what she did at the club. Even if I hadn't been attacked, you don't leave your friend behind. Anger bubbled within me as I stowed my phone and got back to work. I would have to deal with her later.

After lunch, I stood at the circulation desk with my back turned to the lobby. As I organized some returns, a voice said, "Excuse me, can you point me toward the rare collections room?"

I whipped around, recognizing the voice. It was Alaric.

I was pretty sure I looked like an idiot with my mouth agape as I stared at him for far longer than was normal.

"What are you doing here?" I asked.

He smiled at me.

"How did you know I'd be here?" I continued.

"I didn't," he said. "I'm here to do some research in the rare collections room."

I shook my head to remove the confusion. "Of course. What type of research? Is there something you're looking for? I could pull the documents for you."

The blood rushed to my cheeks with embarrassment. Alaric smiled again and approached the circulation desk. He was so close to me now I could practically touch him. My heart felt like it was going a mile a minute.

"I'm interested in examining any literature or historical documents you have that mention vampires," he stated.

"Vampires? That's an interesting topic. You believe in vampires?" I asked, my eyes wide.

"Don't you?" responded Alaric with a smirk.

"Uh, no," I said with a laugh. "Let's see what we can find in rare collections. Come with me." I motioned for Alaric to follow me.

As Alaric trailed behind me, we walked in silence between the stacks as I led him to the rare collections room. While Alaric perused the offerings in the collections room, I headed back to the circulation desk to search our card catalog database for all the documents we had related to vampires. Looking for published work containing vampires was not at the top of my list of things I thought I would ever be researching. At least this minor research project would break up the monotony for an otherwise slow Saturday.

The library had little literature surrounding vampires, but I made sure Alaric had access to what we had. He spent the rest of the afternoon in the rare collections room while I attempted to busy myself and try not to think of him being in such close proximity as me. I had begun my closing duties when Alaric appeared at the circulation desk. He thanked me for the use of the collections rooms and asked to reserve the materials he had been reading this afternoon with plans to return on Monday. Alaric remained standing at the desk, shifting his weight from one foot to the other, like he had something else to say.

"Do you? Uh, would you like to go to dinner with me? Tonight?" he asked.

His sheepish demeanor endeared me. I didn't know what to say. Dinner? Tonight? Of course, I wanted to say yes, but agreeing to a date at the last minute seemed to break some sort of societal rules I should be following. For starters, I didn't know this guy. Yes, he had saved me from being raped, but how did I know he wasn't a creep underneath that charming exterior? He just showed up at my place of work. Was I supposed to believe that was a happenstance occurrence? Despite my misgivings and concerns, my enchantment with Alaric made me want to throw caution to the wind. I took a deep breath, and against my better judgment, agreed.

"I'll pick you up at your flat. Does 7 o'clock work?" asked Alaric.

"I'll be ready," I said with a nod.

And with that, Alaric turned and walked out of the library. I let out a deep exhale and fanned my face. I was going on a date with a mysterious man who was the most handsome thing I had ever seen, with his dark, almost black, brown hair, piercing blue eyes, and tall, muscular physique. It was like I was Goldilocks and everything about Alaric was just right.

I locked the library doors and walked towards my complex. I had just enough time to do a little primping and pick out an outfit for dinner. I didn't know where we were going, so I just went with my typical date outfit, a casual flirty dress that didn't show too much cleavage or too much leg, and flats. I grabbed a cardigan and my clutch before heading out the door. I walked down the path from my apartment to the wrought-iron gate, seeing Alaric outside the gate right on time. He smiled and waved, opening the gate for me as I got closer to him.

"Good evening," he said.

"Hi," I said, smiling at him.

"I hope you like French food," he said with excitement in his eyes..

"I love it."

"I know just the French bistro. Come with me," Alaric motioned.

We strolled down the street, around the corner, and down five more blocks, the street lights beginning to twinkle in the evening dusk. The bistro was quaint and quiet. It was the perfect atmosphere for a first date. The food was exquisite and mouthwatering, as was my date. He was mysterious with a hint of forthcoming. We never ran out of things to talk about, yet Alaric could keep an air of mystery around him. He was just the right amount of commanding and confident without being cocky. As the evening progressed, my nervousness faded, and I relaxed, enjoying his company.

"You sure love French things." I smiled at Alaric, attempting to be flirtatious.

"I do." He smirked.

"Any particular reason?" I asked.

"Well, aside from the language being the most romantic language I've heard, and the food being the best I've tasted, it might have to do with the fact I was raised there."

"That makes a lot of sense," I said, pausing before continuing, "but you barely have an accent."

He chuckled at my realization. "That I don't. I was born and raised in France but moved to London as a teen.

Then, I moved to Massachusetts as an adult. I suppose the accent got muddled along the way. It tends to come out more when I'm angry or speaking French."

"That's cool though. I've always wanted to go to France and England. It's my ultimate dream to visit all the grand libraries."

"Maybe we can plan a trip sometime. I'd love to show you around," Alaric offered.

"That would be wonderful." I smiled.

"So tell me about yourself, Cosette." He leaned back in his chair, looking directly into my eyes. His gaze caused my heart to flutter and I swallowed before answering.

"There's not a lot to know, to be honest. I went to McCallum University for undergrad and graduate school. Then, I got a job at the university library."

"Is your family from here?" he asked.

"No, I grew up in Virginia. My parents are college professors."

"What about siblings?"

"None. Just me, living the life of an only child. What about you?"

"No siblings either. My parents passed when I was a boy, and I've been on my own ever since then."

"I'm sorry to hear about your parents. That must have been hard."

"It was a long time ago," he said, clearing his throat.

Attempting to change the subject, I asked, "What do you like to do for fun?"

"Ah, definitely reading, especially the classics, and talking with beautiful librarians tops my list. And you?"

I giggled. "Beautiful librarians, huh?"

"Well, only one beautiful librarian in particular." We smiled at each other, thoroughly enjoying our conversation.

"I also like to read, if that wasn't obvious from my work profession. I'm a homebody. I love to curl up and crochet, watch movies, and have deep conversations."

"I noticed clubbing didn't make the list. Not your thing, I assume?"

I rolled my eyes. "Definitely not. I only went the other night because my friend Libby wouldn't shut up about it. It will also be the last time I go."

"I have to say I'm happy to hear that. Hopefully, you don't run into any more creepy men."

Our conversation lulled for a moment after Alaric mentioned my assault. Taking a deep breath, I said, "Thank you again for saving me. There's no telling how far that would have gone if you hadn't intervened."

"It was nothing. I'm sorry I brought up such a traumatic event."

"Don't be. I'm glad you were there and that I have someone to talk about it with."

After we finished our meal, we walked down to the river for an evening stroll and took in the sights of McCallum. We listened to the water slapping and lapping at the edges of the shore and smelled the salty aroma of the sea water mixing with the freshness of the tributaries. This was one of the best dates I had been on, and I did not want this night to end. As we reached a bridge overlooking the water, we stopped to gaze downriver.

We stood side to side looking at the water when his hand rested upon my lower back, firm and sure. I turned to look up at him. Butterflies danced in my stomach at his proximity. He turned his body to face mine, gazing into my eyes. I placed my hand on his side as I stared up, mesmerized by his lips. He caught me looking at his mouth and shifted his gaze down to mine. Then, as if in slow motion, Alaric reached up with his other hand to cup my face and angled it towards his. My heart raced in my chest as our faces got closer and closer to each other until he pressed his lips to mine. It was soft, slow, and seductive.

I leaned my body into him, tipping my head up further, opening my mouth, and inviting him in. He responded in kind and deepened the kiss. Our tongues flicked and tangled together before he nibbled and tugged on my lower lip. He pulled away, giving me my lip back, and let out a guttural grunt, murmuring *mon tresor* under his breath. Letting out a breath, he pressed his forehead against mine and tucked my hair behind my ear.

I took a breath and attempted to swallow the lump in my throat. That had to be the best first kiss I had ever had despite my limited experience to compare it to. Alaric continued to look at me, his eyes dark and smoldering. He stared at me like I was the prey he wanted to devour. I moved closer to him with eyes soft and knees weak, willing to be consumed by him.

Alaric reached down with his mouth to give me a smaller, yet sensual kiss. The kiss was beautiful and left me wanting more. He smiled and offered his arm for us to continue with our walk. We strolled along the waterfront in a comfortable silence that one could only experience with someone they have known or been with for a long time. It felt cozy and relaxing to be enjoying each other's company, the night air descending upon us like a cool blanket.

Our stroll concluded when we arrived back at the gate to my complex faster than I had wanted. The evening had gone too fast, and I didn't want the night to end. I didn't want to say goodbye to Alaric or part from his company.

How was it possible to be drawn to this man with such fervor, like a moth to a flame? My mind whirled with excuses to keep this man from leaving.

What was wrong with me? This was our first date and little, old, inexperienced me was dying to invite Alaric up to my apartment and into my bed. I had visualized at least five different positions I wanted this man in, which caused my thighs to tingle and dampness to form between my legs. This was not normal for me, and I didn't know how to make it stop. *Did I want to make it stop?* No, the answer was no. I was attracted to this man and wanted him. Lost in my head, with my thoughts swirling, I didn't realize Alaric was speaking to me.

"I had a pleasant time tonight," confessed Alaric.

"Me too," I exhaled, my voice breathy and seductive.

I shifted from one foot to the other, gazing down at the ground and unable to meet his eyes. Alaric made me flustered and wanting. His proximity to me was intoxicating.

Gathering my courage, I asked, "Would you like to come upstairs?"

I was worried the offer would scare him off or give him a less-than-stellar opinion of me. As I looked into his smoldering eyes, a smile bloomed on his face.

"I would love to," he said.

5

COSETTE

Present Day

I grabbed his hand and led him up the stairs to my apartment. As I fumbled with my keys to unlock the door, he stood beside me, leaning his shoulder against the door frame. His other arm gripped the top of the doorway, allowing his shirt to ride up, revealing his chiseled abs. I couldn't look at him for too long or I feared my heart would beat out of my chest. I took a deep breath as I opened the door, motioning him to follow me.

Once inside, my mind was racing as I attempted to engage in small talk with Alaric. I offered him a glass of red wine before I began giving him a tour of the apartment. One could call my apartment shabby chic, I suppose. Comfy neutrals decorated the space and everything from my furry couch pillows to plush blankets screamed cozy. While I'm not entirely a type A person, my apartment was neat, but lived in. While in my office, Alaric seemed enthralled with the book selection.

"Quite a lot of old books you have here," Alaric said.

"What librarian wouldn't?" I teased.

Alaric studied the bookshelf full of classics, particularly those from the mid-nineteenth century.

"*Anna Karenina, Black Beauty, Around the World in Eighty Days, Alice's Adventures in Wonderland/Through the Looking-Glass…* You have quite the collection."

"Thank you." I smiled.

Alaric crouched down to examine the books closer, plucking *Alice's Adventures in Wonderland* off the shelf before rising to his full height.

"I love that book," I said.

"A first edition? How did you get your hands on this?"

"Estate sale. Some people don't realize the worth of the items their relatives have. I was lucky to stumble upon it."

He touched the front cover with reverence, gazing at the faded red cover. The gold gilt was peeling in places, and stains lingered haphazardly on the front.

"I haven't read this in ages," he said, thumbing through the book.

Placing the book back on the shelf, he continued to peruse the rest of the bookcase and sip his wine. When he was finished, he put his wineglass down and turned to face me. He stared into my eyes, tangling his fingers in my hair. As I gazed up, Alaric pulled me into his chest, close enough to feel the muscles under his shirt. He pulled on my hair to angle my head upward, guiding my mouth to his. His mouth opened, inviting my tongue inside his. Our tongues entwined as he cupped my face. His grip on my body grew harder and more intense the longer our kiss continued. As he pulled me closer to him, he let out a deep growl. I fisted his shirt in my hands, rubbing them over his chest. His hands trailed long lines over my backside, cupping my ass with a possessive squeeze.

I pulled him in even closer, feeling the large bulge at the front of his pants. I let my hands run over his back while grinding my front into his.

"Gods, I want you," Alaric boomed in a husky voice. He yanked my hair even harder while he slammed his mouth into mine. Our tongues tangled and danced together between nibbles on each other's lips. I groaned with pleasure as Alaric made his way from my mouth, leaving quick kisses from my jawline to my ear, giving it a little tug with his teeth. He trailed his tongue from my ear down my neck as I tilted my head to give him easier access.

His kisses felt intoxicating, leaving me weak in the knees. As if he could read my mind, he held more of my body weight in his grip and continued to place kisses from my ears to my shoulders. He pulled back, gazing into my eyes, his hands on my shoulders.

"Is this okay?" he questioned, studying my face for a reaction.

I couldn't answer with words, but gave him a sultry smirk before grabbing his hand and leading him toward the bedroom. He glided his hands up to the string securing the front of my dress, pulling it out of its bow. My dress slid down my shoulders, leaving my porcelain skin exposed. He inhaled as he took in my form in my bra and panties, his eyes searing into me. I fought the urge to cover myself.

"You look beautiful," he said, letting out an audible groan.

He came closer to me, showering me with more sensuous kisses while leading me backward until the back of my knees touched the bed. He guided me to sit on the edge of the bed while he moved to stand in front of me, positioning himself in between my knees.

I gazed up at him while he slipped my bra straps off my shoulders, allowing my breasts to pop free. I groaned as he cupped each breast with his hands, massaging in soft strokes. Alaric rubbed each nipple until peaks formed, giving each one a small squeeze.

He let out a series of soft grunts as he lowered himself to his knees and took a breast into his hot, wet mouth. I arched my back, pressing my breast further into his mouth. He sucked and flicked my nipple with his tongue, sending waves of pleasure through me.

Alaric trailed kisses and licked down my stomach until he neared the apex of my thighs. He moved down to the inside of my thighs, kissing, licking, and sucking. All this attention and teasing made me squirm with desire. I wanted him so badly. He left a kiss on the seam over my panties, and I moaned. The heat of his mouth penetrated through the fabric as he played with my underwear, running his fingers on either side of the gusset, teasing me some more.

Shivers coursed through my body as I ground my groin into his face. I raked my fingers through his thick, dark hair while he continued his marathon of teasing, hooking his index finger in between my sex and underwear, lightly grazing me. The sensation sent electricity throughout my body, and I tugged his hair harder.

Alaric hooked his fingers into my panties, pulling them downward. He gazed up at me with hooded eyes filled with lust. A grunt of approval sounded as he examined my nakedness.

He peppered kisses all around my seam while using his finger to run up and down the length of me. He slid a finger into me and then another. He removed his fingers, glazed with my arousal. Without saying a word, Alaric looked me in the eye as he moved his fingers to his mouth and sucked my juices from his fingers. Eyeing my pussy, his fingers descended into me, alternating between curling his fingers and pumping them into me. As if to tease me, he stilled his fingers and withdrew them, leaving my pussy aching for more.

He smirked while lowering his mouth to run a flat tongue up my seam leisurely. He then turned his concentration to my clit while inserting his two fingers into me again. As he licked and sucked, he curled his fingers, finding my G-spot.

Alaric continued sucking my clit and pumping his fingers into me as I approached orgasm. As my body quivered, he increased the intensity of his licking and continued to pump my pussy until I cried out with ecstasy and shuddered with delight.

Instead of being sated, I wanted more. All I wanted was Alaric, and I was willing to do whatever it took to feel him inside of me. He was standing in front of me as I sat up on the bed's edge. I lifted the edge of his shirt up and over his head, revealing his chiseled chest and a ruby-red amulet around his neck. My hands moved down his abdomen and settled on the waistband of his pants. Unbuttoning his pants and lowering his zipper, he watched me as I pushed his pants down. As he stood in his boxer briefs, I eyed his dick, which was inches away from my face. I looked up at him before hooking my fingers into the waistband. As I pushed his underwear downward, his cock sprung forth. His dick was a beautiful specimen of smooth, soft skin that required both my hands to encompass his length. I could barely contain his girth in my hand. As I stroked his cock, his veins pulsed, engorging further with blood.

I licked my lips with anticipation while looking at his beautiful length. I gripped him with one hand, squeezing him gently, trying to reach my fingers around him. Alaric groaned with pleasure.

"Yes, Cosette. Just like that."

I took the tip of his cock into my mouth, swirling my tongue around his head. Alaric let out a growl while placing his hand on my head. I popped him out of my mouth and licked the underside of him from root to tip.

"Damn, that feels so good. Don't stop."

I slipped him back into my mouth, sucking on him like my personal lollipop, hollowing out my cheeks to take as much of him as I could, pumping my hand around his base in tandem with my sucking. It didn't take long for him to squirm as he inched closer to orgasm. His hips bucked forward as I sucked and pumped him faster. Adding more pressure with his hand on my head, he fucked my mouth with vigor.

"Fuck Cosette," Alaric exclaimed. "You're going to make me come."

I shifted my gaze up to his eyes, continuing my sucking.

"Another time, *mon tresor*," he said, placing his hands on my face to stop me. "I want– no, I *need*, to be inside you," he demanded.

"Alaric," I said breathlessly.

He scooped me up into his arms to move me farther up the bed and laid me down. Alaric hovered over me, gazing at my pussy. He gripped his cock, running it along my seam and over my clit, collecting my arousal. He positioned himself at my entrance. I gulped and swallowed nervously, hoping I could take all of him.

As if he knew what I was thinking, Alaric entered me slowly, stretching me as I embraced the burn of his girth. He rolled his hips, moving in and out of me, inch by inch, until he was fully seated inside me. We moaned and moved together; the ecstasy growing as Alaric pumped in and out of me vigorously.

As we kept rhythm with each other, I pulled Alaric closer to me, sucking his tongue in my mouth. He slowed his pace, supporting my head from behind with his hands, while continuing to roll his hips. He kissed me and as he pulled back, we made eye contact with each other. We continued watching each other as we approached orgasm. Seconds later, an orgasm crashed over me. While my body continued to have aftershocks of pleasure, Alaric felt his release and collapsed on his side next to me.

We laid in silence, catching our breaths, letting the endorphins wash over us. Turning to my side, I ran my fingertips over his chest, fingering the necklace that hung around his neck. The chain had a rope-like design with a dark red ruby surrounded by filigree embellishments suspended from it.

"It's beautiful," I commented, holding the oval in my hand.

"Thank you," Alaric said.

In the afterglow, Alaric said little. He adjusted his body so that the amulet was out of arm's length from me. I wasn't sure if it was deliberate on his part or if he was regretting the end of our evening.

"It's a family heirloom," he said, clearing his throat.

I had never dated a man who wore jewelry, but from what little I knew about Alaric, I would say it was fitting. The amulet intrigued me. It seemed more than just a sentimental family heirloom. I wondered if there was more to it than that.

6

ALARIC

1873

Opening my eyes revealed the wooden beams of Rosie's cottage. For a moment, I couldn't recall how I got to her home or why I was there. The rust-colored stains on my hands alerted me to what had transpired in the mere minutes before I had passed out.

The memories, emotions, and shock rushed back. My gaze panned over to see Rosie's lifeless body on the ground, close to my own. She was limp, cold, and paler than I had ever seen her. Dried blood covered her naked body and added dark streaks to her red hair.

My thoughts raced, making it difficult to focus on my next step and my stomach churned with a queasiness I had never encountered before. I couldn't leave her here, but I couldn't stay in her cottage or this town. Burying Rosie was the only respectable and logical thing to do.

I knelt beside Rosie, gathering her body in my arms, cradling her close to me, palming her face, and turning it toward mine.

"Rosie, *mon tresor*, I'm sorry. I never meant to do this. Please forgive me, my love." While sobbing, I laid her on the bed and examined her clothing in the wardrobe. It wouldn't be right to bury her naked.

I fingered the different fabrics of her dresses, stopping to admire one. It reminded me of the first time I laid eyes on Rosie. The town had hosted a dance, and she appeared, wearing this elegant gold dress made of shimmering silk. The bodice had accentuated her curves without being indecent. She had worn it with an ornate sash draped around her middle. It had made her fiery hair and delicate features grab my attention.

Redirecting myself from the memory, I gathered the dress in my arms and laid it down beside Rosie. I cleaned her body as thoroughly of blood as I could, attempting to restore her hair to its original glory. Piece by piece, I fitted the gown on Rosie. Even in death, she was breathtaking.

In a stiff back chair, I sat by Rosie's bed for what seemed like ages. I stared and admired her, contemplating how I was going to do this. It was impossible to comprehend how I was going to bury my fiancé. Killing wasn't what I had in mind for this evening nor a middle-of-the-night burial. *How does one go about doing this?*

I struggled to catch my breath, my chest heaving and my hands dripping with perspiration as I attempted to sort out a plan. There was no one I could talk to or who could assist me, so I gathered my courage and marched outside to the gardening shed. I traipsed through the foliage, needing to go far enough to hide a newly dug grave, but close enough to carry Rosie's body through the terrain without tiring.

After trekking a mile from the cottage, I began digging a burial site in the damp earth. With only the light from the lantern, I worked for hours. Wiping the sweat from my brow, I looked at the grave with plenty of room to lay Rosie to rest in a dignified manner.

Satisfied with her resting spot, I hiked back to the cottage to begin the last portion of my plan. Along the way, I stopped briefly inside Rosie's greenhouse. She loved gardening and flowers, and it was full of beautiful, blooming roses. The aroma of the greenhouse instantly reminded me of the hints of rose petals in the perfume she usually wore. I snipped a few blooms; roses for my Rosie. When I got back to the cottage, I wrapped Rosie in a blanket from her bed.

Speaking to her as I did in life, I placed the roses on her chest and lifted her into my arms like a sleeping child. Carrying her through the kitchen and out the back door of the cottage, I set out to take her to her ultimate resting place.

Trudging through the dark forest with my arms full and a lantern turned into a much more laborious task than expected as I hiked through the crisp foliage on the ground. It took far longer to walk the mile to the site, as I had to stop several times to rest. Exhausted and gasping for air, I laid Rosie down at the edge of the grave.

"Oh, my darling. I am sorry everything ended this way. You trusted me and that loyalty took you from me. I will feel forever guilty for allowing you to have that much belief in me. Thank you for loving me, Rosie, even if it was but for a short time. You are the love of my life, Rosie. There will never be another. I love you."

I wanted to tell her I thought myself a monster, and all I could think about was killing myself just to be with her in whatever afterworld she was in.

Picking Rosie up, I lowered her into the hole using her blanket and admired her from above. How peaceful she seemed, as if sleeping. My red-haired version of Sleeping Beauty. I sobbed.

The time had come. I scooped a shovelful of dirt, feeling the rough handle of the rusty shovel and let the dirt fall softly into the grave. I continued shoveling the ground back where it belonged. My speed and intensity increased as the sobs and tears flowed.

As the sun peaked above the horizon, it cast golden hues through the tree branches as I laid the last scoopful of dirt on the grave. I drew in a breath, exhaled, and walked in the direction of the cottage with the shovel and lantern in hand.

I turned to her resting spot one last time and said, "Goodbye, Rosie."

7

ALARIC

Present Day

Sex with Cosette had been unexpected, yet amazing. We laid side by side, catching our breath. Her light brown hair was tousled, with bangs in her eyes, and the bottom of her hair grazing her nipples. I draped my arm around her waist, drawing her closer until our bodies were touching. My hand slid up to touch her cheek while I ran my thumb over her bottom lip.

She looked up at me with those blue doe eyes, searching my face. I leaned in and kissed her gently. As I deepened the kiss, my hands trailed along her body, and I nibbled at her bottom lip. As she pushed her body against mine, she moved her hand down my torso, causing my pelvis to jerk toward her instinctively.

Cosette giggled at my reaction. With a smile on my face, I planted a kiss on her forehead.

"I didn't expect this to happen tonight," she said.

"Me either," I said.

"I'm happy that it happened, don't get me wrong. I didn't want you to assume this is my usual first date routine."

"You'll get no judgment from me. I couldn't have waited another minute," I said, gripping her ass.

"That's good to know. I'm assuming this won't be a one-night stand then." She grinned slightly, her head bent toward the floor. She fidgeted in the pause before my response, her nervousness on display.

"Definitely not. Doing it again can't come soon enough."

I didn't want to scare her off, but I was ready to fuck her brainless. I'll have to exercise patience. *Slow and steady wins the race, Alaric.*

Knowing Cosette for only a short time didn't deter me from the powerful feelings I was already developing. I needed to be careful of my urges though and how I managed them around Cosette. I couldn't afford to get carried away feeding on someone I was developing serious feelings for. Despite it being such a long time ago, I couldn't stomach her fate becoming the same as Rosie's.

I thought back to her being attacked in the alley, rescuing her without hesitation. In just a few minutes, I was mesmerized by Cosette. Seeing her in the library by mere coincidence had confirmed my budding feelings. Upon sight of her, my heart leapt in my chest and beat faster the closer I got to her. I was beginning to love everything about her.

Her hair, the perfect length for running my fingers through and for grabbing during a romp in the sheets. Eyes that pierced through my shell-like exterior that I had worked hard to cultivate. Just as her beauty drew me in, so did her intellect and our shared love for research and reading. Our chemistry in and out of the bedroom wasn't something I could ignore. Somehow, this woman had brought feelings of excitement and trepidation within me, something I hadn't experienced in quite some time.

Cosette stood up, draping a silken robe from the bedside chair around herself. "Would you like some water?"

"Yes, please. I'm parched."

As I waited for Cosette to return, I laid in bed with my hands behind my head, gazing at the ceiling, and daydreamed about her. I was captivated after one date. How? She didn't know the real me or what I was. Would she be open to me or run away from my true self?

"Here you go." Cosette said, handing me a glass of water.

After gulping down half the glass, I placed it on the nightstand before turning over. "Now, what do you think we should do next?" I eyed her seductively.

Cosette broke out into giggles.

"I hope you're ready for me, *mon tresor*, because this time, I will not be gentle." Her eyes widened. "I can't wait to have you screaming my name as you come. I'm going to mark every part of your body as mine."

Cosette swallowed, unable to speak. The look of shock traveled across her face.

"Which of your openings do you think I should start with first?" I asked with a wink.

"First?"

"I don't want to frighten you, Cosette, but eventually I will have you in every way possible."

"But I'm….not experienced..." She hesitated, looking down at her hands.

"Don't worry, I didn't say it all had to happen tonight. We can talk about what you're comfortable with and the rest can wait until you're comfortable. Okay?"

"Okay." Cosette looked reluctant. I needed her to trust that I wouldn't do anything until she wanted to. Learning she was inexperienced wasn't a shock. This wasn't about fucking for me, it was about my feelings for Cosette. When the time was right, I'd let her know the truth about me and my feelings for her.

"Where were we?" I tucked an errant hair behind her ear.

"You were just about to ravage me." Cosette smirked.

I grinned. "You don't have to tell me twice." As my statement sent Cosette into a fit of laughter, I moved my body to hover over hers, pulling the bedcovers over us.

***

Sunlight poured into Cosette's bedroom Sunday morning, casting a warm glow upon her face. She had slept peacefully in my arms all night. I wanted nothing more than to continue watching her sleep curled up next to me.

Cosette let out a sigh before rolling onto her back and murmuring, "Morning." She smiled at me, content.

"Good morning." I leaned down to give her a kiss. "How did you sleep?"

"Amazing."

"Me too. I could sleep for ages curled up next to you."

I smiled at her, being a vampire meant my body didn't require sleep and for a century and a half my senses caused a level of hypervigilance that made it nearly impossible for me to relax enough to fall asleep. But having Cosette in my arms put me at such ease that I had been able to sleep soundly for the first time in ages.

"I'm not complaining," she joked.

I squeezed her even closer to me, unable to keep my hands off her. The more I touched her, the more I felt my cock hardening.

"Someone's awake and ready to go," Cosette said, regarding my expanding length.

"I can't help it. You have this effect on me."

Without a word, Cosette covered us with the blankets to hide from the world. Neither one of us seemed to be able to keep from touching the other. We laid there for a long while kissing and talking until Cosette's stomach grumbled so loudly we couldn't ignore it.

"I suppose we should do something about that stomach of yours. Let me cook you breakfast." Cosette smiled at my offer before we both rolled out of bed and made our way to her kitchen.

I searched for what I could scrounge together in Cosette's pantry. While cooking, I found myself lost in my thoughts. I realized it had been several days since I had last fed. The gnawing feeling of hunger was becoming harder to dismiss. It surprised me to learn when I became a vampire that I could still eat human food. However, it no longer nourished me like animal or human blood did. Eating human food was just to keep up appearances.

Plating the food jolted me out of my thoughts. *"Bon appetit, mon tresor."* I said, setting the plate before Cosette.

***

After breakfast, we said our goodbyes. I needed to feed before I made another mistake and killed someone out of hunger. I took my time walking back to my apartment from Cosette's. Coming home to my little charming nook brought a smile to my face. I wanted to bring Cosette here, but I'm sure she wouldn't react well to jarfuls of blood.

I opened the fridge and removed a jar. After pouring the contents of the jar into a saucepan, I warmed it on low heat. When it had reached the perfect temperature, I poured the blood into a wine glass. Animal blood wasn't perfect, but it would do in a pinch. After gulping down the contents, I wiped my mouth before continuing to clean up the mess in the kitchen.

That night, as I laid in bed, I ached to have Cosette beside me and my body burned to touch her again. I replayed our date and our first night together in my head. My hand went straight to the bulge in my pants, rubbing from root to tip, imagining Cosette doing it. As I pictured her riding me and grinding her nub into me, I slid my hand into my pants, gripping the root of my increasing erection. I stroked the length of my cock lightly, redistributing the drop of pre-cum onto my shaft on the downward stroke.

The memory of being in her mouth almost made me explode. And gods, whenever I get to take her ass, I know it will be the most glorious feeling. I gripped harder and faster with each pass of my shaft. The tightness in my lower abdomen grew as my balls crept closer to my body. I rolled my thumb over the tip of my cock, stroking with such intensity and clutching my girth so hard it was almost painful. The tempo continued to increase, and I felt my climax grow until I erupted with Cosette's name on my tongue and my contents spilling out of my hands.

8

ALARIC

1873

Surrounded by Rosie's belongings at the cottage only compounded my grief. I knew I couldn't stay long for multiple reasons. The longer I lingered, the more likely I was to join Rosie in death at my hand or someone from the village would discover what I had done.

I looked around one last time at Rosie's cottage, letting my fingers trail over the surfaces, and touching the fabrics of her clothing and her bed. My hands gripped the bed sheets and, shoving my face into them, I inhaled the last remnants of Rosie. Her scent would always be with me.

Closing the door to the cozy bungalow, I left Rosie's for the last time. My thoughts consumed me. I couldn't focus on where or what I was doing. My thoughts bounced between memories of Rosie, of us together, and of making love to her before I had killed her.

I wandered around the village all day and into the evening until I found myself at the entrance of the tavern. Returning to the same location that had been the starting point of last evening seemed ironic and yet, fitting. I couldn't think of anything else I'd rather do to placate my guilt than drown my sorrows.

Meandering to the bar area, I made eye contact with the barkeep and ordered myself a pint of ale. I sat at the bar, knowing I needed more than one round of alcohol to help me forget. Staring into my fifth mug of ale and lost in thought, a woman approached me and sidled up next to me at the bar. Not bothering to raise my head, I stared at the mug of ale in front of me in between sips.

"Alaric, I haven't seen you in ages," she greeted.

I faced the familiar voice and realized it was Mary. She was a buxom brunette I had briefly courted before meeting Rosie. "Hello Mary," I said glumly.

"How are you? Where have you been?" She chatted aimlessly until she noticed my current state of mind. "Goodness, Alaric. What's bothering you?"

What was I supposed to say to her? It's not like I could confess to her I'm a vampire and I killed the love of my life. Lying had never been a strong suit of mine, so a half-truth to Mary was as good as she was going to get. "My engagement was broken off," I managed, shifting on my stool while swirling my mug of alcohol.

"Oh, darling," Mary comforted, leaning in closer to my face and grazing it with her fingers. "That is the absolute worst. I do hope you aren't too heartbroken."

"I am rather devastated," I confessed. "The only way I know to console myself is with alcohol." I chuckled to diffuse the situation.

Mary smiled. "I can think of some other ways to console you."

Or someone, I thought. Mary wanted to be the one to console me and help erase the pain. I wanted to forget and was feeling the effects of the ale. I inquired, "What did you have in mind?"

Acting entirely too pleased with herself, Mary placed her hand on my shoulder and with a light squeeze asked, "Want to get out of here?"

In response, I downed the contents of my mug and gestured for her to lead the way. In my depressive state, I had nothing left to lose. We left through the back door of the tavern and headed down the alleyway. I felt the tug on my thoughts relent briefly as I felt Mary's hand slip in mine.

For a brief moment, it was as if nothing in my life had changed. Rosie and I were walking hand in hand down the street. As quickly as the illusion had descended upon me, it dissipated with realization.

My heart pumped faster, and I felt the buzz of attraction. That tiny spark that feeds into lust, want, and desire. I wasn't doing this to get over Rosie. It was a distraction, something to numb the pain. We walked hand in hand until we reached the doorway of Mary's apartment. Talking wasn't a priority for either of us. I wanted to forget, and she wanted to feel.

Mary led me by the hands through the doorway and without saying a word, reached up, planting a kiss upon my lips. I returned it with very little vigor, resulting in Mary pulling back from me. With a questioning look, she asked, "Do you not want this?" She searched my eyes and I could tell she was hoping she was misinterpreting my actions.

Instead of answering, I gently pulled her to me and kissed her. My head and my heart didn't want this, but my body, my biology, and my vampire-self craved this. I was grateful that Mary looked nothing like Rosie; I didn't think my emotions could withstand it if she did. We kissed in the main room of her apartment. Kisses of two people who barely knew one another and those who were reacting to their physical whims. Kisses that were unlike the passionate ones I had just experienced with Rosie the night before.

Mary caressed her hands delicately up and down my limbs. I tipped my head back and stood still, allowing her to continue her attention. She leaned in again to kiss me. Looking into my eyes, she slowly unbuttoned my vest, one button at a time. I shrugged off my vest, and she assisted with removing my shirt over my head. Mary stood back, admired my body, and smiled. She trailed her hands over my chest, then lower to my abdomen, and finally, she traced her fingers over my waistband.

I stood in front of her, watching her. Looking me in the eye, Mary skimmed her fingers just inside my pants. The act sent a tingling sensation throughout my body. Mary fixed her eyes on mine as she left a trail of kisses from my chest to my lower abdomen. She unbuttoned my trousers and let them fall to the floor. My cock sprang forth, showing my arousal. A small groan escaped my lips as relief flooded me from the release of the confinement of my trousers. Mary looked at my length, her eyes widening, and then seductively licked her lips.

Shifting her gaze from mine to my cock, Mary lowered herself to her knees. She took my girth in her hand and ever so gently licked the bead of pre-cum from the tip. The sensation sent a shutter throughout my entire body. Sensing my continuing arousal, she pressed her lips around the head of my cock. Hollowing out her cheeks, she sucked, lightly at first and then with such intensity I thought I would come immediately.

I tipped my head back in pleasure and Mary slowed her pace, teasing me, sliding her tongue up and down my length. She rose, gripping my ass with both her hands. She led me to the edge of her bed, motioning for me to sit. Kneeling on the ground in between my knees, she smirked before palming my balls in her hand, giving them a small tug before turning her attention back to my cock. She placed the head of my cock back in her mouth, sucking with fervor, drawing more and more of my cock into her mouth with each pass until she had taken me to the hilt.

I was about to explode with pleasure. Feeling the tension growing in my belly and the tightness in my balls and ass, I let out an animalistic growl. As if sensing my impending release and not wanting our evening to end, Mary popped my cock out of her mouth.

She stood and undid her corset, teasing me while untying her laces, one eyelet at a time. I sucked in a large breath after she let her corset fall, revealing her voluminous breasts. Admiring her curves, I watched as she dropped her skirt to the floor and stood naked before me.

Feeling I could not wait a second longer, I grabbed her wrists and pulled her closer to me. Mary remained standing while I peppered kisses up and down her abdomen, stopping to press my hands on her tits. I could barely contain the soft volume in my hands as she made groans of her own that made my cock twitch.

Palming her in my hands, I stroked each breast until both of her nipples formed stiff peaks. I took my time popping each one into my mouth. She moaned as I coaxed her legs on to either side of my thighs so that she was straddling me. Her wetness seeped onto my length, telling me she was more than ready.

I could feel arousal building up within me while I grabbed my cock and ran it through her slit, coating myself in her juices. Then, without another moment's hesitation, I lined myself up with her opening and slammed inside. She took me to the hilt as she let out a cry of pleasure.

Grabbing her ass, I guided her up and down my cock, stretching her and ending each stroke with a slam, giving her my entire length. As my arousal increased, I continued to take and take. I was no longer concerned with her pleasure as I chased my orgasm. With my last strokes, another type of desire burned within me.

Before I knew what was happening, my canines elongated and plunged deep into Mary's neck. She cried out in shock and horror as I held her down and fed from her. After a few sucks from her, my orgasm radiated through me.

Continuing to drink from her, I realized it prolonged my orgasm and feelings of arousal. It took all my strength to stop myself. I pulled her body away from me, prepared to plead for her forgiveness, but as I examined her face, I realized my nightmares would continue. Mary's head bobbed loose as I noticed the telltale paleness and limpness of her body.

I had killed again.

9

ALARIC

Present Day

Monday morning, I rose early to prepare for my day at the library. It would be full of research, but also an opportunity to see Cosette. I hoped I would find out more about my maker and my kind, but I wasn't sure what I was looking for exactly.

Over the past 150 years after I became a vampire, I've spent much of that time searching for answers. Each lead I found would end without fruitful knowledge. Despite this, I continued to come to the library, searching for new information.

"Good morning," Cosette said with a smile as I entered the library.

"Morning," I greeted.

"I've already pulled your sources and placed them in the special collections room for you."

"Thank you. Would you be able to escort me? I'm afraid I don't quite remember how to get there," I said, coyly staring up and down her body.

I suspected she knew my true motive but she walked past me and led the way to the room, humoring me. Thank gods it was secluded and in a low traffic area of the library. She opened the door and I brushed past her into the room before turning to face her. Placing my hand on her arm, I pulled her into my embrace and let the door swing shut. "Finally," I said, kissing her.

The first kiss was friendly enough, but as I deepened the kiss, Cosette returned my affection. I pressed us against the collection's room door, nudging her back with my hands on her waist. Moving my hands to her ass, I slipped my tongue into her mouth. Cosette ground her pelvis into mine, begging for more.

Hungry to taste her, my kisses slipped from her mouth and down her neck. She moaned, and it only encouraged me to continue peppering her with kisses and touches down her body.

"I need to taste you. Now," I said.

"Someone might see us," Cosette worried.

"I don't care. Let them watch for all I care."

Cosette gasped as I palmed her breasts over her shirt and made my way down to her skirt. She was the spitting image of a stereotypical sexy librarian with her pencil skirt and a top she paired with a cardigan. My hands roamed downward, over her ass, giving it a little squeeze, and then further down her skirt. Her skirt firmly in my hands, I pulled it up and over her ass until it gathered around her waist. With her lacy underwear on display, I trailed my fingers up between her thighs until they met her apex. Rubbing her with my fingers over her panties made me rock hard.

I circled my finger around the gusset of her underwear and ripped her panties downward, so quickly I almost tore them entirely. "Gods, your pussy is beautiful."

Cosette was already breathing heavily with anticipation, her chest rising and falling rapidly. I moved my face desperately close to her slit without touching her, close enough for her to feel my warm breath on her pussy. I wanted her so wet she wouldn't be able to wait another minute longer.

I slid my finger into her folds. *"Mon tresor,* your pussy is soaked. Are you ready for me?"

She looked into my eyes with desire, "Oh, God, yes."

My fingers slid into her drenched pussy, making her moan with desire. I curved my fingers upward, sending her into a fit of pleasure. It was arousing to watch her enjoying her own bliss.

Her noises sent me over the edge. I laid my tongue on her pussy, loving how she tasted, and the feel of her velvety skin. Once I had thoroughly worked her up with my hands and tongue, I stepped back and stood up.

"Lock the door," I whispered in her ear.

"What?"

"Lock. The. Door. Cosette." My eyes darkened as I growled. With a grin, she turned around to lock the door. With her skirt still tangled around her middle, I led her over to the table. "Bend over," I said.

I guided her until her front pressed against the edge of the table and directed her with my hand to lay her torso on the table. Gods, she looked exquisite bent over with her ass in the air. I'd love to take her ass like this, but the library was not the place for that.

In one swift motion, I removed my belt and undid my pants, allowing my length to spring forth. Standing in between Cosette's legs, I lined my cock up with her folds. I slammed into her, not worrying about being gentle. With my hands on her hips, I fucked her hard and rapidly. Cosette's muffled moans of pleasure and our skin slapping together fueled me to continue. It wasn't long before I exploded within her, laying my torso on hers with exhaustion.

I kissed her back as I slid out of her. She turned around and straightened her skirt, and I placed a kiss on her lips.

"Well, that was a surprise," she said, her cheeks red and her breath rapid.

"I hope it was a good one." I smiled.

"I'd say so. Today is the best workday ever," she said with a giggle.

"Glad to be a part of it."

"You should probably get to work on your research."

"I'm sure you have other patrons who need your help."

"None quite like you."

"I can be quite needy."

"Let me know if I can do anything to help you...with your research, I mean." She blushed as she ran her hands through her hair, smoothing it down.

"In all seriousness, I could use your help," I said.

"I'd be happy to. Just let me know what you need."

"Can you search for references on vampires in your available works?"

"I can definitely do that. Let me see what I can dig up in our catalog."

Cosette ran off to do some research while I concentrated on the documents in front of me.

Cosette

Present Day

With Alaric reviewing the documents in the special collections room, I returned to the circulation desk to start my research. I wondered why Alaric was adamant about studying vampires. What did he stand to gain from knowing this? It wasn't common for someone to be investigating a topic without a reason behind it.

The library catalog displayed some additional books that hadn't appeared during my first pass of inquiry. They were in a secluded corner of the library, far from the special collections room, and Alaric. I let Libby know I was stepping away from the desk, and trekked to the forgotten shelves.

Following the library's classification system, I found the text I had been looking for, the *Tome of Immortal Shadows*, in the medieval folktale section. The book was heavy, bound in a sepia-toned leather cover, aged from weather and use. A simple design was used for the front cover, with intricately embossed gold writing displaying the title. The tome's pages were made from parchment and felt rough to the touch. The writing inside was penned with an exquisite and elaborate script made using a quill and ink from a bygone era. Drawings throughout the book were mesmerizing, with others equally terrorizing. With the age of the tome and its contents, I was bound to find something of use from this text.

I spent the rest of the morning looking through the ancient text, attempting to decipher it and gain understanding. Alaric remained sequestered in the collections room and didn't seek me out. By lunch, I had learned a few things and dispelled a few rumors according to the text.

"Daylight doesn't harm vampires. Did you know?" Alaric said.

He had snuck up behind me in the study corner, startling me. "You nearly gave me a heart attack." I clutched my chest.

"My apologies. I didn't mean to scare you."

"And yes, that was one of the few things I came across this morning. Must have been a rumor that vampires can only be out at night and would die in the daylight. Did you come across anything regarding feeding habits?" I asked.

"Not much, just what we know already about feeding on humans. Nothing new there," he replied.

"Well I found something," I flipped to a section in the book I was reading. "They can eat food," I said with surprise and excitement in my voice.

"So you're saying that human food does nothing for them, but they could keep up appearances by doing so?" Alaric surmised.

"Exactly. What about the process of making vampires?" I asked. "This text refers to the term 'maker' and states a vampire must bite and feed upon a human until they are close to death to make another vampire. In order for the transformation to be complete, the body must be drained of blood before the victim turns into a vampire."

"Interesting," he said. "The texts I reviewed also had similar passages. I also read that makers do not hang around once a human turns into a vampire, leaving them to figure it out on their own."

"Wow, that's the definition of a vampire for sure."

"These texts definitely do not give up information freely. Most of the ones I reviewed were vague and mysterious."

"Isn't that why there's such a mystique around vampires?" I questioned. "I would expect any written work on vampires to be that way."

"I suppose you're right," Alaric agreed.

"Why the fascination with vampires anyway?"

Alaric froze at my question and stalled his answer. "Mostly for academic purposes. I enjoy researching how the academic and folklore angles come together to form myths and evolve through history. The cultural histories that tie into the folklore creation of vampires are particularly interesting," he said.

"So you're an academic? I'm surprised you didn't mention it before."

"I try to limit discussing my work topics as most people find them too unbelievable or that I'm crazy for choosing such a topic."

"I can see why you would shy away from volunteering that information. For what it's worth, I find the topic fascinating and I would enjoy hearing more about the angle you're approaching your project from."

"I'd love to show you more. We could work together on it. Your research skills are far superior to mine."

"Deal," I said.

"Did you find anything else that piqued your interest?"

"Actually, I did. This text." I pointed to the *Tome of Immortal Shadows*. "It points to its origins in a small village outside London." I watched as Alaric's eyes widened. "I looked into the village, and it no longer exists. It seems it was swallowed up by London as it grew over the last century."

"What was the name of the village?" Alaric asked.

"Sumner," I replied. He didn't respond to my answer but nodded his head in understanding.

By the afternoon, Alaric finished his research for the day and prepared to head to his apartment. Before he left, he pulled me into a secluded corner, kissing me thoroughly. I was out of breath and lightheaded when he finally pulled back. It took all I had to hold my body upright–this man could kiss. We didn't have a definitive plan to see each other again, but I knew it wouldn't be long. I'm not sure I could take the burn I was experiencing for him much longer.

After work, I headed home to my apartment, ready to relax. I was tired and wanted to crawl into bed with a book and a mug of tea. Sipping my drink, I heard a scratching noise outside my apartment. I rose to investigate, suspecting it to be an animal or something else that was easily explained. but there was nothing outside my bedroom window.

Scratch, scratch.

I heard it again. I walked around the apartment and I checked the other windows. Nothing.

Scratch, scratch.

Where was that noise coming from? It was driving me crazy. I moved toward the balcony sliding door when a pounding rapped on it. A dark figure crept on my balcony, scratching with some type of instrument. Someone was trying to break into my apartment.

Seeing the figure sent me into a frenzy of terror. I backed away from the sliding door, not wanting to turn my back. The figure would break through the glass at any moment. I stepped backward until I reached my bedroom.

My ears perked when I heard a sharp, high-pitched shriek accompanied by a series of brittle cracks of the glass. Soon, this man would find me. I ran to the only place I could think of, my closet. I made myself as small as possible, huddled in the back corner, desperately trying to not flinch or scream with each noise.

I heard the sliding door open casually with a speed as if the man lived here. Boots made heavy footsteps as the figure walked around the apartment. Slow steps echoed down the hallway toward my bedroom. I held my breath as the door to my bedroom was smashed in.

"You can't hide forever. I'll find you," he jeered.

Curling myself into a ball, I flinched when I heard the intruder's voice. My pulse raced and the sound of my blood rushed in my ears as my entire body convulsed with adrenaline. The closet door flew open and my clothes were flung aside. The man reached into the back corner, grabbing my arms and pulling me towards him.

"I told you; you can't hide from me forever."

"Go to hell," I fumed, struggling to get out of his grip.

His grip tightened and he threw me onto the bed. He started to tug my pants off. I kicked and screamed for him to stop, but I couldn't escape him. My pants ripped as he tried to shove my panties down my legs. Dizziness blurred my vision and my hearing devoid of any sound. I struggled to get away, kicking, jerking from side to side, but he squeezed his hands around my neck and choked me. I could feel my movements and fighting becoming weaker with each moment that passed. *He was going to kill me.* It was my last thought before the vision went dark.

A cracking noise reverberated through the apartment, followed by a loud bang, bringing me back to the present. The attacker removed his hands from my neck briefly, allowing me to get in a few more hits and kicks. A booming voice filled the room, and I felt my attacker yanked off me.

"Get the fuck off her."

Alaric. Alaric was here. *How did he know I needed help?* I cried as relief flooded over me. Alaric was here.

10

ALARIC

1873

I had to get out of London. Rosie was gone and Mary was dead, both by my hands. Becoming a vampire had become increasingly detrimental to my life. If I didn't leave, I would be killed or thrown in prison. There was little time for me to plan my escape.

Contemplating where I should go, I sprinted to my flat to gather my meager belongings. I struggled to think of a location because I knew the next place I landed needed to be large. Somewhere I could get lost in the throng of people, but also a place I wouldn't mind spending months or decades. Somewhere I could start anew.

England and France were off the table, considering how close-knit the European social networks were. Living in some of the smaller villages along the coast, far away from London, crossed my mind, but England was too small to provide the distance or size I needed to avoid detection. I would have loved to return to my birthplace of France, but again, it wasn't far enough for me to feel comfortable in my anonymity.

In my flat, I opened my world atlas and turned to the page featuring America. The move involved crossing an ocean and being more than a world away from the home I had known for twenty-eight years.

I had a country. Now, I needed to determine a city that would fit my needs. Considering many cities, I decided to stick to the east coast.

Loving bustling cities, I gravitated toward Boston, but it didn't seem like the right fit. After examining the map, I honed in on a city close to the Massachusetts coast. McCallum would be my new home. It was sizable enough to obscure my identity and any future vampire activity I did in the future. With my decision made, I set about planning my move.

***

The next morning, I found myself on the *Starlight,* bound for McCallum. The ship was not a luxury liner, by any means, but I would be comfortable for the three to four-week journey. I wasn't thrilled about spending that much time on a ship in the middle of the Atlantic Ocean and hoped the weather and tides were in my favor. My presence on the ship as a new vampire was another concern.

Before I left for America, I collected several jars of animal blood, hoping to stave off the urge to feed. I had only been a vampire for a few days, so I didn't know if animal blood would satisfy my craving the way human blood did. If I was going to survive this voyage, I couldn't feed off the other passengers on the ship, even if I managed to not kill them.

As the ship departed port, I stood on the main deck, resting my arms on the railing. My thoughts drifted to and fro, from Rosie to memories of my childhood in France and back to the events of the past couple of days. I closed my eyes, pressing my fingers to my eyelids to relieve the pressure. Emotion had drained me, so I retreated to my cabin, hoping to forget all that had happened. Looking toward the future was my only means of survival.

I had to forget.

One Week At Sea

"Shit," I murmured as the last drops of animal blood dripped onto my tongue. *What was I going to do now?* The blood had barely kept my cravings in check and now, only one week into my voyage, I was out. I was going to have to work out something before I had another craving.

Don't panic. You can figure this out.

I crept down the hall, nodding to the steward, before taking the stairs to the main deck. The evening moonlight lit the deck in shadows as I prowled around the ship, contemplating my next move.

During my stroll, a dark-haired beauty walked aimlessly from the ship's railing to the benches and around the deck. Drawn by her good looks, I followed her below deck and into the ship's saloon.

She sat at the bar, spirit in hand. I hung back, observing, before having a seat at the opposite end of the bar. This woman was breathtaking in her red dress and her ebony hair swept up to show off her long neck. Attempting to control myself, I licked my lips at the sight of her and her thrumming pulse.

Gathering courage, I stood and walked to her end of the bar. "Is this seat taken?" I asked.

"No," she said, demurely. She paused for a moment before a coy smile grew on her face. "I was wondering when you would come say hello."

My eyes enlarged to the size of saucers. "You were?"

"Of course. I noticed you following me around on the main deck."

"You did? Forgive me, I hope I didn't unnerve you. I was captured by your beauty and thought you looked mournful walking around like that."

"No harm done," she reassured me. "I'm not sad, per se, more so lonely. I'm traveling alone and find myself secluded aboard the ship."

"Isn't it frowned upon for young ladies, such as yourself, to travel unaccompanied?" I asked.

She smiled. "It is. But I found myself in a rather unsettling situation back in London and I needed to leave rather quickly."

"I see," I said as I swirled the cocktail in my hand. We sat in comfortable silence for a few minutes. Admiring her beauty, I extended my hand to formally introduce myself. "My name's Alaric."

She shook my hand. "Annie."

"It's a pleasure," I said.

Annie looked down into her drink as she swirled the glass in her hand. All the while, a sensation engulfed my body and my hands began to tremble. *Oh no, not again. Not another craving.* I had just finished my last jar of animal blood. It had lasted less and less each time.

Noticing the change in my demeanor, Annie asked, "Alaric, are you okay?"

Attempting to swallow the lump in my throat, I gulped and inhaled slowly. I couldn't answer her question for fear I would lash out or lose the last thread of control I had.

Annie placed her hand around my bicep, saying, "Here, come with me. Let's get you back to your cabin."

I nodded in agreement.

"Tell me your cabin number," she said.

"423," I replied.

We scurried through the ship until we reached my room. Once inside, Annie turned to me with confirmation in her voice. "You're a vampire, aren't you?"

I stared at her. "Wh..wha…what?"

"You're a vampire. I'm guessing you haven't been turned for very long. You're trembling. How long has it been since you last fed?" She asked as she looked around the room, her eyes landing on a few jars I had rinsed out and left to dry on the counter.

Shock had disoriented me to the point I forgot not to reveal my secret. "How did you know?" I asked.

"Let's just say I have experience with your kind. And I know if you don't feed on a human soon, you're either going to die or most likely, kill someone."

I hung my head with regret.

"Let me guess, you've already killed someone."

Holding up my fingers to indicate, I said, "Two, actually."

Annie sighed, closed her eyes, and paced around the room. "Here's what we're going to do. You're going to feed off me to quench your cravings and then you'll repay me by assisting me with my needs."

"Your needs? What are those exactly?"

"Sex. I want, no, *need,* to be fucked."

Two Weeks At Sea

My cabin was silent aside from the sucking sound of my feeding and Annie's moans. While I sucked her femoral artery, my right hand massaged her clit, eliciting louder calls of passion. Removing my mouth from her groin, I placed my other hand over her lips.

"You keep that up and someone will find us," I said.

Annie reached up to remove my hand so she could speak. "I'm sorry, Alaric. I'll be quiet, I swear."

"Yes, you will, or I won't fuck you the way I know you want." I warned as she mewled and squirmed in my hands.

From the start, it was clear we both had needs that weren't being met. She needed sex, and I needed blood. It didn't hurt that I appeared to be getting the better end of the deal-even if the sex wasn't as fulfilling as I liked. She was a stranger to me; no strings attached and no emotions to trip me up.

I was still adjusting to vampire life, but I realized I could use it to my advantage. Annie knew she couldn't divulge my secret, or I'd kill her. I wouldn't hesitate to do so to protect myself as we crossed the ocean.

After I finished feeding, I sat up on the side of the bed while Annie fidgeted in her heightened state of arousal. She gave me her sexiest stare, and she said, "Where's my reward?"

She was trying to be coy about it. "What do you want?" I asked in a flat tone.

"You." She smiled and attempted to kiss me on the mouth.

I moved so that she missed and landed a kiss on my neck. Warm, tender displays of affection weren't part of our deal. She knew that.

"What. Do. You. Want. Annie?" I was getting annoyed and wouldn't continue to entertain this arrangement if it weren't for being stuck on a ship with no other means of obtaining sustenance.

Annie placed her hands on my chest for a moment before moving them down to my pants. I could tell where she wanted this to go, and I wasn't in the mood for a lackluster dick sucking. "Annie," I said, tilting her head upwards, so we were eye to eye. "We're not doing that tonight. What do *you* want?"

"Fuck me."

Attempting to contain an eye roll, I said, "As you wish." I flipped her over onto all fours. Besides the no kissing rule, I also didn't have sex face-to-face. Not after Rosie. Sex was no longer about emotion and attachment. This was me just holding up my end of the bargain, nothing more. Once we both had reached the pinnacle, I dismissed Annie as nicely as possible. I locked the door behind her and settled in for the night. As I lay in my bed, processing all that has happened in the past few weeks, guilt swept over me. I felt like I was living my own worst nightmare. I had killed not one, but two people who certainly did not deserve what happened to them. Figuring out a way to control my urges had to be a top priority from here on. I couldn't continue to kill innocent people. As a human, I prided myself on having moral character and as a vampire, I wasn't living up to my own standards. This had to stop, or I wouldn't survive.

One Week Later

The *Starlight* docked in Massachusetts after three weeks at sea. I was thankful to be on dry land and for the speedy voyage. Annie and I bid *adieu* to each other on the deck before the gangway was assembled. At the first possible moment, I exited the ship to lose myself among the throngs of people.

I hesitated in my movements around McCallum, paranoid Annie would follow me wanting to continue our arrangement - or worse, divulge *what* I was. Walking around McCallum solidified my decision that this was the right place for me. While it was a growing city, it also had a quaint feeling that reminded me of my childhood in France.

Before searching for a place of my own, I needed to find lodging to recover from the journey and plan my new life here. I found a boarding house run by a no-fuss, middle-aged woman named Mira. It was nice to stay somewhere private despite it being temporary.

Three days later, I moved into my apartment.

11

ALARIC

Present Day

Perched in my desk chair, I had resumed my research for some time after returning to my apartment. While sipping my glass of blood, unease and panic gripped me. I couldn't breathe as the terror coursed through my body.

This awareness within my body was new to me. The hair on my neck prickled, and my extremities tingled. The sensation in my gut told me something was off, something was wrong. It told me I needed to check on Cosette. I couldn't pinpoint how I knew it was about Cosette, but I listened.

I didn't waste time trying to call her. Instead, I rushed out of the apartment, breaking from a jog to a full-on run to Cosette's apartment, ten blocks away. Upon arriving at her door, I heard screaming and crashing from inside. I kicked in the door, splintering the door frame, and charged towards

Cosette's screams. Back in her bedroom, she thrashed on the bed, a figure hovered over a half-naked Cosette.

Before I could control myself, my fury consumed me. My canines elongated, and my rage engulfed the figure on top of Cosette. I grabbed the back of his shirt and pulled the figure off Cosette, slamming him against the wall. Stunned from the impact of the wall, the figure hesitated long enough for me to grab him. While clutching his hair, I forced back his head and plunged my fangs into his jugular. His hands scraped and clawed at me with little vigor. I was going to drain this motherfucker. No one. And I mean no one touches *mon tresor*.

The attacker's body went limp, any sounds he made diminished as I fed, and after I drained him, I eviscerated the vessels in his neck. Examining the body, the attacker was a mid-twenties looking man with dingy blonde hair. His eyes displayed the vacant stare of death with his neck vessels and sinew splayed in all directions.

During my rage kill, Cosette had screamed with fright and scrambled to escape from the room. The apartment was now silent. Now that the attacker was beyond resurrection, I searched the apartment to find Cosette cowering near the front door. She was so frightened she screamed when I entered the living room.

Still out of breath, I realized how I must look to her with my blue eyes wild amd full of residual rage. My heavy breathing sounded like a crazed madman accompanied by the growls of an animal. Specks of blood dotted my hands and a stream of blood remained on each corner of my mouth. While my fangs had retracted, my clothing was ripped and my hair was a wild, tangled mess.

Slowing my breathing, I attempted to rein in my rage and formulate thoughts. Here laid another kill at my feet. But this time, I had no remorse. Cosette was mine, and I wasn't about to let some scumbag sully her.

In the living room, Cosette cowered in her half-naked state. Her hair was matted, and her arms draped around her body. Whether she was chilled or trying to cover her nakedness in front of me, I wasn't sure. She exhaled with terror in her eyes.

"Cosette," I said, trying not to scare her further, approaching her slowly.

"Get away from me! Don't touch me!" She scrambled further away from me until her back hit the wall. With nowhere left to go, she slid down to the floor, curling up in a ball.

"I will not hurt you."

"How do I know that? You're a vampire?!" Her face was wild with terror.

Her intonation told me she was both accusing me and questioning her assumption. Hearing Cosette say aloud what I am was both my salvation and the source of my trepidation. She was the only person, alive and in this century, who knew my secret now. My stomach churned with relief and anticipation.

I lowered myself to a crouching position, hoping she would still accept me. "I am a vampire, yes. I wouldn't hurt you, Cosette, because you are mine."

"Yours? What does that even mean? I don't belong to you," she scoffed, scrunching up her face in disgust at my statement.

"It means," I hesitated, "I love you."

"You *love* me? I don't *know* you. You lied to me. I want you to leave!" She stood from her crouching position and stalked one step toward me.

"Cosette..." I pleaded.

"Get out Alaric. Leave! Never talk to me again!" She commanded, pointing to the door, her face red with anger and stoicism.

I stalked to the door, turning to speak to her before she slammed it in my face. Her body thumped against the door, and I heard her slide down while she sobbed.

I stood on the other side of the door, paralyzed and unsure of what to do next. My heart felt like it was suffocating, like it couldn't beat for anything but her. I couldn't lose Cosette like this. I hadn't decided to tell her I loved her.

It just came out. It was the truth, though. I loved her. She was the person for me, the person I was always supposed to be with. I couldn't explain to myself or others why I did, I just had this deep instinct in my gut. This feeling that completely consumed me and wrecked me down to the core.

I gazed at the broken door frame. The door's frame required repairs for security. Concern swept over me as I thought about how Cosette's attacker had known where she lived. The bar incident appeared to be a random act, making the subsequent attack even more perplexing. It didn't add up. *Was it a break and entering gone wrong or perhaps a stalker? Perhaps it was someone from the library or the bar?* My mind swirled with possibilities.

Revealing myself as a vampire to Cosette wasn't in my plans, but the moment I saw the man attacking her, I lost all inhibition. No one touches Cosette like that, but me.

How can I get her to talk to me? She had kicked me out with a dead guy in her apartment, and I still heard her sobs coming from inside.

I knocked on the door. "Cosette, let me in, please."

Silence.

"Talk to me, please. Let me explain."

Silence.

I pressed my ear against the door, listening for any movement inside. "I'll tell you everything, Cosette. Anything you want to know. I won't hurt you. Ever," I begged, desperation in my voice. I rolled my back against the building and used the hem of my shirt to wipe the blood from my face.

The door cracked open enough for me to see one red-rimmed, tear-stained eye. She sniffled and stared at me.

"Can I come in, please?"

She didn't answer, but opened the door wider to allow me to walk past her. Relief washed over me while I hoped Cosette would be open to hearing my explanation. As she sat on the couch, she held a knife defensively in her hands.

"Go on, talk," she ordered, her face revealing no emotion.

I sat on the chair opposite her, clasping my hands together and resting my elbows on my knees. Raking a hand through my hair to calm my nerves, I said, "Okay, wow. Where to start?"

Crossing her arms, she said, "The beginning. I want to know everything. And don't you dare lie to me."

She was uncomfortable in my presence now and angry with me for concealing who I truly was. I reached for her with my hands, wanting to hold her, but I lowered them, thinking better of it. "I never wanted or meant to lie to you, Cosette."

"The beginning, Alaric," she huffed.

I drew in a large breath and exhaled. "I was born in France, but lived most of my life in a tiny village outside London. Sumner; the village from the book you found in the library." I paused and closed my eyes. As I exhaled, I opened my eyes and continued.

"I became a vampire in 1873, at 28 years old. I didn't know the vampire who was my maker. He didn't stick around to help me." I drew in a breath with a quiver in my jaw. "I walked to my fianceé's house, where I killed her in the heat of passion." I inclined my head to meet her eyes with tears trickling down my face.

"My control wasn't stellar then, as I was a new vampire. Her death almost destroyed me, and I was lost for a long time because of it. I couldn't stomach being in London any longer, and I came to America. I ended up here in McCallum." She remained silent, watching me wipe the tears from my face, desperate to put myself back together. "I've been on a quest for information about vampires, my maker, and anything relevant."

Cosette stared at me without saying a word.

"I realize I gave you a quick rundown. I'm happy to answer all the questions you have. I would never hurt you, Cosette. I love you."

She stood up, drawing in a large breath. "I don't know what to say, Alaric. It's a bit much to process."

"I understand. I didn't want to keep it from you, but I was afraid you would freak out. It's hard to confess to others that you're a vampire, so I haven't confided in anyone other than for my survival needs."

"Ever?"

"Never. Just hadn't met anyone I trusted or wanted to tell until I met you."

"What about your life before you became a vampire?" She said as she paced around the living room.

"What would you like to know?"

"What about your family? Your parents? Did you have siblings?"

"No family now, of course. But my family wasn't big back then either. It was just my parents and I until I was eight."

"What happened when you were eight?" Cosette asked.

"My father came home ill one day from his job at the factory where he worked. His cheeks were flushed. He had a fever and a cough. We thought he had some run-of-the-mill illness until my mother developed the same symptoms. Less than a week later, I was an orphan."

Cosette stopped her pacing. "Alaric, that's terrible. I'm so sorry."

"I realize now they had tuberculosis. It was miraculous I didn't develop it too, considering how contagious it is."

Cosette peered down at her feet. "What happened after your parents died?"

"I lived in an orphanage until I was thirteen, when I ran away to live in London."

"I can't imagine how terrible it must have been for you. It seems like a rough life to lead."

"It wasn't easy. I worked all the menial jobs I could find at that age. They were not the most glamorous jobs. But I worked hard, taught myself all the subjects I needed to know to go to university."

"What did you major in?" Cosette asked, intrigue in her voice.

"History," I said with a smile.

"How fitting." She gave me a genuine smile. She paused, considering all I had told her. Then she asked, "How did you know I was in trouble?"

"I'm not sure. This was the first time it had happened. I got this weird prickly sensation on the back of my neck. It had an ominous feel to it. I had a feeling you were in trouble, although I can't explain why. I ran as fast as possible. When I got here, you were screaming, so I busted in the door."

"Okay. I'll no doubt have more questions, but your necklace is all I can think about right now. Is that a vampire thing?"

I picked up the amulet and moved it along the chain on my neck.

"I guess you could say that. My fiancée, Rosie, gave it to me when I showed up at her cottage as a new vampire. She said it would give me protection."

"What kind of protection?"

"All I know about this necklace is what Rosie shared with me. I was looking to gather more information about that aspect through the rare books. I have found little though. I don't know where it came from or its full protective capacity."

"So how do I know you won't kill me, even if you don't mean to?"

I thought about her question. She was worried, and I wanted to reassure her. But even with years of experience, I couldn't make that promise. "I understand your worry, and I would never do anything to harm you, Cosette. Making a promise like that as a vampire would be foolish, I know."

My hands went to my neck to remove the surrounding chain. Holding it out to her, I said, "I want you to have this. It will protect you from harm. Harm from me or from any other vampires while you wear it."

"Don't you need the protection?"

"No. And I'd rather you be protected. This is my promise to you, Cosette. If you wear this necklace, no harm will come to you."

Cosette pulled it over her head, pulling her long hair through and positioning the amulet on her chest. She was quiet for some time. I knew she had questions swirling in her head, but I wanted to give her space to work through her thoughts at her own pace. Remaining across from her, my own thoughts flowed in and out of my consciousness.

"I thought of something else," she said.

"Ask anything you want."

"How many people have you killed?"

"Since becoming a vampire? Five perhaps?"

"You don't know?" Cosette said with shock on her face.

"To be fair, it was a long time ago. I killed people as a new vampire because I didn't know when to stop feeding. The only people I have killed intentionally were the men who attacked you."

Silence.

"And I didn't want to kill them. It's like my body goes into autopilot mode when it comes to you, and I can't control myself."

Wrapping her arms around herself, Cosette asked, "How do I know you can control yourself around me and not kill me? I'm just supposed to depend upon a necklace for safety?"

"There are other things that can help," I offered.

"Like what?"

"While I prefer to get most of my energy from human blood, I can use animal blood to fill in the gaps between cravings and live human donors."

We sat for a while as I let her take her time. I didn't want to rush her, but I hoped she would still want to date me. Lifting her head, she studied me. "I think I'm going to need time to think about this."

"I understand. Take all the time you need. I'm not going anywhere."

"I appreciate that. I'll call you."

"That sounds amenable. Before I leave, I'll take care of…" I didn't finish my sentence but gestured to the dead body in her bedroom.

"Oh, yes. That would be helpful. I don't have any experience disposing of dead bodies." We both let out small chuckles despite the circumstances.

"Let me fix your door as well. It's only the door frame. The lock is still intact." I gave the door another once-over.

"Yes, thank you," Cosette agreed.

I made quick work of moving the body unnoticed out of Cosette's apartment while she readied herself for bed. Then, I took a piece of wood from her bathroom door frame and attached it to her front door frame.

"This should work for now. I can come back later this week to fix it and your bathroom door frame, too."

"Thank you, Alaric. I appreciate it."

We both stood in silence for a few moments before I continued. "Are you sure you're going to be okay by yourself?"

"Yes, thank you. I'll be fine."

"I'm only a call away if you need me."

"Goodnight, Alaric," she said as she closed her apartment door and left me to walk home.

12

Present Day

I wanted to trust Alaric, despite my brain telling me to run far, far away. There was no way I was going to sleep tonight between flashbacks of a dead guy on my floor and all these thoughts swirling through my head. I tried to sleep but was left tossing and turning in my bed.

Eventually, I gave up and went to the kitchen. Rummaging around in the fridge, I grabbed handfuls of snacks to shove in my mouth. At least I could pretend to eat my way to the answers I was seeking. As I crunched on some chips, I contemplated what I knew about Alaric, and what I knew defied all logic. He had fangs. Before my very eyes, I saw him use them to drink blood from my attacker. He mysteriously showed up at the club and then the library. It all just seemed far-fetched and too coincidental.

Alaric was a vampire and a killer. He killed for me, to protect me. I didn't know how to feel about him or the situation. It wasn't like I could tell Libby or anyone else about my situation. They would think I was crazy, and it would endanger Alaric. However, I wasn't sure if I still wanted to protect him. My mind and heart were at odds as my heart told me to keep caring, but my head remarked on how stupid that notion was.

If I were to believe him, the necklace should protect me from him and other vampires. I never thought I would need protection from immortal beings and I hoped I would never need the security the necklace afforded. Hell, I wasn't sure I could trust the necklace did what Alaric said it did either.

There was a lot I didn't know about vampires, about Alaric, or why I was attacked. What I knew was he sensed I was in trouble and came to save me. If he had wanted me as food, he could have fed from me the instant he saw me. But he didn't. Instead, he seemed to care for me and appeared relieved once he had confessed the truth.

Moving on from the chips, I nibbled on a muffin while I fired up my laptop. While the academic information on vampires appeared limited, I wanted to see what the good ol' internet could drum up.

I plugged keyword after keyword into the search engine with little result. Searching for vampires on the internet was futile as all that came up were fictitious creations and pop culture references. Finally, in the depths of the internet, I stumbled upon a relic of a website–the type of site that was created and hadn't been updated since the early 1990s. It was cryptic and mysterious. That seemed to be the going theme when it came to vampires.

The further I delved into the website, I started to come across familiar topics. Much of the information on the site was similar if not the same as the references Alaric and I had found in the library. Then, the word "ruby" caught my eye.

Doing a double take, I slowed my skimming to a halt. All of a sudden, I was reading about a ruby amulet; a necklace that strongly resembled the one Alaric gave me, the one hanging around my neck. The description was brief and confirmed the protective quality Alaric had referenced.

I sat back in my chair, thinking over my little internet deep dive. It was all too much to digest. I felt nauseated with conflict, my thoughts pinging around my brain. Needing to get out of my head, I wanted to get someone else's opinion on this whole situation. I had to trust I was making the right decision in telling someone else. It was late, but there was one person I knew I could text. Libby.

Cosette: You up?

Libby: Of course. Question is…why are you?

Cosette: Can't sleep. A lot on my mind.

Libby: Well I'm assuming you texted me for a reason. So spill!

Cosette: It's about a guy.

Libby: Ooolala! Cosette has a man?!

Cosette: Hush..and yes? Maybe? So I met this guy and we've been having sex...

Libby: Okay, you have my attention.

Cosette: I can't quite pinpoint it, but I just have this nagging feeling about him and I'm not sure I should continue to see him.

Libby: How did you meet this beefcake?

Cosette: At the club. Well, outside it. He saved me from being assaulted and escorted me home. You know, the night you DITCHED me? Don't think for one second I'm not still pissed about that.

Libby: I had hoped you had forgotten about that. This guy sounds nice and gentlemanly. I don't see the problem.

Cosette: I realized he'd been keeping secrets from me, which I confronted him about. He fessed up but now I worry he will continue with the secrets and lying.

Libby: I'm not going to lie, I'm not a fan of liars.

Cosette: Me either, but he seems to have come clean and he seemed relieved to finally be telling me the truth.

Libby: And the sex is?

Cosette: Mind-blowing. Earth-shattering. Orgasmic. Need I continue?

Libby: Girl. Stop right there. You need to ride this out (pun intended). Do not stop, do not pass go. Let your little bookworm self enjoy this time in your life. Even if this ends up being a fling, you need to get yourself some while the gettin' is good.

Cosette: So you think I should continue seeing him?

Libby: Yes! For fuck's sake, yes! Ride that man into the sunset and then climb him like a tree! Text him and have his fine ass come over and do you right!

Cosette: Thanks for the vote of confidence, Lib. I might actually follow your advice this time.

Libby: You better, and tell me every detail.

Cosette: You wish. Thanks for the pep talk. I'm off to bed. Night.

Libby: Night.

I gave my conversation with Libby some serious thought. She made some interesting, yet logical points despite not knowing the entire story. Still conflicted, I ran through all my thoughts again and again.

Against my better judgment, my heart was winning out this tug of war with my mind. Why my heart was determined to forgive Alaric and embrace a relationship with him, I didn't know, but I was tired of fighting it. Choosing to embrace my feelings for Alaric just felt right.

The next morning, I sent Alaric a text.

Cosette: I'm ready to talk. Can we meet after work today?

Alaric: Sounds great. Where?

Cosette: Your place?

Alaric: Perfect. 7 pm?

Cosette: I'll be there. Send me the address.

Alaric: 1611 York Blvd, Apartment 1A

Cosette: See you at 7.

***

All day at work, I tried to keep myself busy. What possessed me to think going to a vampire's *lair* was a good idea? Every fifteen minutes I had to talk myself out of a panic attack, reminding myself this wasn't the 1800s and it was an apartment, not a lair. At the thought of seeing Alaric again, my palms started to sweat, my face flushed, and the rest of my skin felt clammy. Every time I thought about my plans for the evening, my pulse raced and my breathing became erratic. There was no reason to be afraid of Alaric. Right?

I worked until after six, so there was no time to head home. Work-chic Cosette was all Alaric was going to get this evening. I didn't know how long our conversation was going to last, so I swung by the deli nearest the library to snag a club sandwich and some vegetable soup.

After picking up my food, I headed to York Boulevard. Alaric's apartment wasn't far from the library and looked like a building straight out of the mid-1880s. It had that vintage, historic charm old buildings from that era have. After finding apartment 1A, I knocked on the door and waited for Alaric to answer the door.

He answered a beat longer than I thought it should have taken him, making me question whether he was at home. When he opened the door, his hair wet and wavy, and a towel wrapped around his waist. I gawked at his naked torso, as I watched the rivulets of water run down in between his muscular abs. I must have shown my surprise as he said, "I promise I didn't plan to answer the door like this." He smirked.

"Uh-huh, sure," I said.

"I promise. The afternoon got away from me when I realized I hadn't showered today, and you would not appreciate the way I smelled."

He saw my dinner in my hand, gestured for me to come in, and directed me to the kitchen. "Make yourself comfortable. I'll be right back."

I assumed he was going to put clothes on because if I had to stare at him half-naked all evening, there would be no conversations to be had. He returned moments later, leaning his upper body, now clad in a sweater, on the kitchen island while I finished my food.

"So," he said.

"So," I said, clearing my throat. I was nervous about having this conversation. "I'm sure you're curious why I wanted to talk to you."

"I have a guess, but the floor is yours."

"I've given everything a lot of thought since last night. I think I am okay with everything. I'll have more questions along the way, I'm sure, but the things that are most important have been shown to me. You saved me from being raped twice. You say you love me. As far as I know, you haven't lied to me about anything else unless it pertained to you being a vampire, and I assume that you have been honest with me since."

"Right. I will always save you. And yes, I love you. I know that may feel sudden, but I know it's you I want to be with."

"Did you feel this way about Rosie?"

He paused a beat before continuing, "No. My relationship with Rosie was different. It was the 1870s and life was different back then. Relationships were different. I loved Rosie, but I never felt this way around her as I feel when I'm around you. It may be because I am a vampire now and I wasn't when Rosie and I first started courting. I'm not sure."

"What happened to Rosie?"

Alaric took in a big breath and exhaled. "She died. I came to her after I had been turned. She took me in, nursed my wounds, and offered me protection by giving me the necklace. We had never been intimate before. It wasn't something you did before marriage then. That night, we took things farther than they had ever gone before and I got carried away. I ended up draining her and killing her. I had to bury her near her cottage and leave the area for fear of getting killed."

"That's terrible."

"It was, which is why I would never let myself do that to you. I always want to protect you. I promise to be your protector, always."

I smiled while fiddling with the necklace. Leaving my chair, I rounded the island to embrace Alaric with a hug. As I pulled back from the hug, I looked up into his deep blue eyes, searching in them for anything other than the truth they held. I stretched up to give him a kiss. He bent his upper body downward to accommodate my stature and drew me closer with his arms around me. I ran my hands through his damp hair as he leaned me into a slight dip and deepened the kiss. The kiss was passionate and needy, requiring all my restraint to not strip all of his clothes off right this instant and worship his body with mine.

Alaric had the same thoughts as he grasped the back of my thighs to lift me up level with him and carried me straight to his bed. He stood at the edge of the bed with me still in his arms. My legs wrapped around his torso and our lips never parted. When we were both frantic for more, Alaric bent down to lay me on the bed.

One would have thought I was as fragile as porcelain the way Alaric put me on the bed. He kissed me with tenderness, brushing his hands over my body. I moaned as he continued to deliver pleasure everywhere he touched. His delicateness with me was short-lived as he growled in response to my moans. Touches became firmer, needy, and insistent. Alaric grunted with his own pleasure as he worshiped my body.

"Your body is amazing, Cosette. Everything about you is incredible," he murmured in my ear. "It's like you were made for me."

He continued laying kisses down my neck while he ran his hands under my shirt. I raked my hands over his back and underneath his sweater, tugging it over his head. This man was beautiful, and he made me feel the same. My desire for him consumed me, making it almost unbearable.

"I want you, Alaric."

His eyes darkened, and he growled. It was all the confirmation he needed to remove my clothes posthaste. He sat back for a moment, looking at my nakedness. Alaric licked his lips, which only made more juices collect between my legs.

As Alaric ran his fingers along my apex, he said, "I see you're ready for me."

Damn, his smirk was enough to make me open my legs and let him do whatever he wanted to me.

Removing his belt with one hand and popping the button of his jeans with the other, he quickly removed them and his boxer briefs. This left nothing but his erection on display. My lips parted at the sight of his cock.

"I know what you're thinking, *mon tresor*, but I have other plans for us tonight."

I laughed. "I'm not sure if I should be scared or excited."

"I like you a bit of both," he teased.

"So, tell me about these plans you have for us tonight." I grinned at him.

"What don't I have planned? I want to lick and kiss every inch of your skin. We'll be fucking so loud even the gods will hear us."

I had no response to what he had said. I was beyond turned on by his words and could visualize every moment of ecstasy in my head. "What are you waiting for?"

My giggling set him off to a frenzy of activity. Grabbing my thighs, he pulled my entire body down the bed and closer to him. Before I could formulate thoughts, he was primed and ready at my entrance.

"I know you're ready for me."

"Yes," was all I could whisper.

He thrusted into me in one swift motion. It was shocking and pleasurable all at the same time. Alaric wasted no time rocking us together at a steady pace. He altered his pace, slowing as he peppered kisses all over my lips. He withdrew his cock, flipping me over onto my knees.

"Grab that rail," Alaric instructed as he nodded toward the bed rail.

"Yes, sir," I giggled.

With his hands on my hips, he directed me in line with him. He slid his cock up and down my slit, coating it in my juices. This time, he drove into me harder and faster before eliciting a deep moan from my parted lips. From behind, he angled deeper into me and the sound of our skin slapping together caused me to yell, "Harder!"

As he pounded into me, Alaric began rubbing his finger in between my butt cheeks and around my asshole. This was unfamiliar territory for me, but something I was excited and desperate to try with Alaric. I never knew having a finger in such a taboo spot would cause me so much pleasure. I found it hard to concentrate on both sensations as he drove in both my lower holes. Holding on to the bed rail, moans and sounds of bliss erupted from our mouths.

Alaric's body tensed and I knew he was getting close to climax. Without warning, he removed his cock and positioned me back on my back before sliding back inside me. We resumed kissing and rocking together at our previous pace. He pulled his lips away from mine and, suddenly, Alaric's canines elongated.

"Bite me." I said, surprising even myself that I had uttered those words.

"No," Alaric said sternly.

"Come on, Alaric. I want you to."

Alaric stopped moving. "Cosette, I can't. I'm afraid I'll hurt you."

"No, you won't. Plus, I have your necklace." I grabbed the ruby around my neck.

"You trust me that much?"

"I do. I trust you'll know when to stop."

Alaric stared into my eyes. I could tell he was contemplating if he should feed on me. He would never think to ask this of me. But I was dying to know what it felt like and knew I could only entrust this to him.

Alaric nodded and positioned his mouth over the side of my neck. Hovering over my neck, he asked, "You're sure?"

"Yes." I breathed.

My consent confirmed, Alaric plunged his canines into my neck, sucking furiously. Despite the initial sting of the bite, I felt no pain and found Alaric feeding from me to be very erotic. His sucking slowed, and he lapped at the pooling blood. As he licked the small drops of blood trickling down my neck, Alaric resumed thrusting in and out of me. Our bodies slapped together with increasing speed until we both reached the precipice of release before tumbling over the edge together.

Basking in our post-sex bliss, we lay together, catching our breath. Blood trailed down the corners of Alaric's mouth and dried on my neck. I nuzzled into his chest and we lay in bed together for a long time before mustering up the energy to clean ourselves.

***

After washing myself, I stepped out of Alaric's bathroom to see him sitting on his bed, clad in gray sweatpants and nothing else.

"Are you okay, *mon tresor*?" he asked.

"Yeah," I said, standing in front of him and gazing down to meet his eyes.

He reached up to delicately rub my arms in an up and down motion. "You sure? I didn't hurt you? You weren't afraid?"

"No, I told you. I trust you. You're not a new vampire anymore. I know you know how to control yourself now."

His thumbs migrated upward to run over my bitemarks. "You put a lot of trust in me. I guess I'm still taking the whole experience in."

"Me too. I think I liked it...like a lot."

"You did?" Alaric asked, hope in his eyes.

"Yes," I said, shifting my eyes downward and grinning sheepishly. "I didn't think I would like it that much, but the whole experience really turned me on and I felt closer to you, emotionally. I know that's a really girly thing to say." I felt the warmth come to my cheeks as I blushed.

Alaric cupped my face and pulled me gingerly to him for a kiss. "I think…that is the perfect thing to say. I feel the same way."

"You do?"

"Yeah," he said, with a smile. "I was so afraid of hurting you or losing control. But I realized I needed to trust myself, just as much as you trusted me. I've never done this with anyone besides you. Sexually, I mean. Since Rosie, it's always just been for sustenance or a biological reaction, not a means for pleasure for myself or for another's."

We both paused, lost in our thoughts, before Alaric added, "I love you, Cosette."

"I love you too," I said, giving him a kiss. Then, with a look of greed and excitement, I asked, "Want to do it again?"

13

ALARIC

Present Day

As I rolled over in bed the next morning, I wrapped my arms around Cosette's middle and drew her closer to me. We lounged for quite a while, listening to the falling rain on the window. I nestled into the crook of her shoulder, running my face along her neck and in her hair. She smelled divine, and it made it impossible for me to get out of bed.

"Let's just stay like this all day," I said.

"I wish. I have to work and you have to...," she trailed off.

"I have my research to do."

"Right."

"But it doesn't mean we have to get up right now," I said with a smile.

Cosette nuzzled her backside into my front.

"Be careful how you do that, *mon tresor*, or you won't be going to work at all," I joked.

Nothing but giggles came from Cosette. We relaxed in bed, dozing on and off until she had to leave for work. With a sensual kiss at the apartment door, Cosette left. I planned to continue my research in the rare collections room for most of the day. Arriving at the library, I gave Cosette a quick wave as I passed the circulation desk and headed to the room. She had pulled all my research items, and they were waiting on the table for me.

I had been in the collections room for quite some time when a tingling sensation arose on the back of my neck before it quickly evolved into goosebumps. Attempting to put myself at ease, I covertly tried to assess my surroundings for anything amiss. When my clandestine attempt revealed nothing, I chose to search around further for the cause.

Venturing out into the library, I perused the stacks, enjoying each shelf of books while on the lookout for anything out of the ordinary. I wasn't searching for any particular book, but I needed a moment to collect myself and a break from the monotony of my research, anyway. I had always enjoyed the scent of a library and reveled in the quiet.

As I meandered back by the special collections room, I glimpsed a figure in my peripheral vision. The shadow was slight, wearing an emerald colored floor-length dress. I stalked closer to the room to gain a better vantage point. A woman studied the contents of the collections room, including my resources on the table and my notes. I inched closer to the door without making my presence obvious. As I positioned my body at an angle, the woman turned a fraction to reveal long curly hair.

I gasped at the red hue. As my brain connected all the dots, the figure turned and I let out a breath as she spoke.

"Hello, Alaric," she said coldly from the doorway.

My jaw dropped. I couldn't form words. My mind couldn't believe the truth my eyes saw.

"I've missed you," the red-haired woman said as she took three steps into the room.

I didn't know what to say. I kept staring at her, unable to move. Panic stirred inside me and my stomach churned. At last, I collected my thoughts enough to utter, "Rosie."

I swallowed the lump in my throat as I looked at her. Rosie. *My Rosie*, stood here in front of me, 150 years later. A rush of emotions swirled inside me as old feelings of love and admiration trickled into my surprise. She really was standing right in front of me with the same red ringlets and petite frame. Conflicted by the sight in front of me and the emotions battling within me, I asked, "How? How are you here?"

"The same way you are," she replied as she moved within arms distance of me..

"What do you mean?" I asked.

She sighed. "Do I really need to explain this to you?" She paused, and then let out a huff. "You bit me, fed on me, and boom, I woke up a vampire."

I paused for a moment, letting the information wash over me.. "So that would make me…"

"My maker, yes," Rosie replied, crossing her arms over her chest.

"Oh gods. But I thought you were dead." I ran my hands through my hair before resting them on the top of my head and spinning my body around in a circle.

"I sort of was, I guess. I'm not entirely sure how the whole process works."

"So you're looking for answers?" I nodded towards the table with my research on it.

"I guess you could say that." She fingered the materials on the desk.

"That makes two of us," I muttered.

I stared at her as she smirked and strode around the room. She turned to face me.

"You've been busy," she said. "I've had my eye on you. You've been working hard looking for something in these ancient books. I wonder what that could be?"

By the end of her question, she was nearly nose to nose with me. Looking at Rosie, I continued to listen to her, trying to understand her endgame. Unease rippled through my body as she returned to stalking around the table. Her behavior told me she was after something; this was not my Rosie from the past, this Rosie emanated an aura cold as ice.

"Why are you here, Rosie?" I said coldly, my voice devoid of emotions.

She gasped as she placed her hand on her chest, feigning shock.

"Didn't you miss me after the last 150 years, Alaric?"

"*Miss you?* I have been *devastated* for the past 150 years! I had to bury your body. Living with the knowledge that I killed you almost caused my own demise. After all these years, I find out that I made you a vampire! It's all too much to take in at the moment."

Rosie slinked around the table and approached me again. Laying her hand on my shoulder, she spoke. "Oh, sweet Alaric. Have you tortured yourself all these years? Release those harrowing thoughts." She made a gesture with her hand as if she was waving away any bad thoughts. "I'm here now and we can be together for eternity."

I shrugged off her advances with annoyance. "Rosie, I can't start over with you. Too much time has passed. We are both two very different people. And most importantly, I have someone in my life now."

"I know," she said matter-of-factly and straightened her spine.

"You know?" I took a step back, deep fear rattled through me.

She grinned. "Of course."

"If you're aware I'm with someone, why are you talking about us being together?"

She advanced toward me again, pointing her index finger at me. "Because Alaric, I had you first. You promised yourself to me. We sealed ourselves together before you turned me. We are destined to be together for eternity."

I couldn't begin to comprehend what she had just said. "Wait, how did you know I was in a relationship?"

Rosie grinned with a glint in her eye. "I've had my eye on you for quite a while. It took me 150 years to find you, and I wasn't about to let your location be lost to me again."

My thoughts wandered to my brief time in London before moving to McCallum. Why had it taken Rosie so long to find me?

"You could do better," she said.

"Excuse me?" My eyes widened.

"I've seen your little girlfriend and you deserve much better."

"What do you mean, you've seen her?"

"I have my ways," she said, a mischievous smile slithering across her red lips.

I approached her until I was near enough to see every pore on her face. "Rosie, I don't know what you're getting at here, what you want, or how you know what Cosette looks like, but it needs to stop."

"Cosette…what a fitting name," she smiled, smugly.

I scowled at Rosie, crossing my arms. "What's that supposed to mean?"

"She has the same appearance, the resemblance of a peasant. She's just so…plain."

I grew more and more irritated each time Rosie mentioned us being together. I pushed aside any warm, tender feelings that had surfaced. I threw up my hands in front of my body.

"Okay, Rosie, we're done here. I don't know why you're looking for me or what you want, but I have nothing for you." I threw my hands up in the air, waving her away.

"Pity. We could have been so powerful together. It's a shame Carl couldn't finish the job."

"Carl? Who the fuck is Carl?" My voice raised in volume.

She laughed.

"Rosie, I demand to know what you're talking about!"

"Alaric, you're no fun. I'll let you use that intellectual brain of yours to figure out who Carl is."

I couldn't believe I used to love this woman. She spoke in riddles, loving every minute of it. The entire conversation infuriated me, and I was in no mood to play games. I knew I was repeating myself, but I felt I needed to be firm in my stance to her.

"Rosie, I don't know why you're here, what you want, or how you found me and Cosette, but it needs to stop *now*. Leave me and Cosette out of whatever it is."

She said nothing as the smirk remained on her face, like she was in on some horrifying secret I was not. Her presence was suffocating; I needed to get out of this room, out of this building, and away from Rosie. She was up to something and I had to protect Cosette from her-at all costs.

14

ALARIC

Present Day

I left the library feeling unnerved following my encounter with Rosie. It was all too much to comprehend. Cosette needed to know about everything, but for now, I needed to wrap my head around it first.

Squeezing my eyes shut, I attempted to suppress my racing pulse and clenched my jaw at the thought of telling Cosette that Rosie was alive, as alive as a vampire could be. Rosie seemed hellbent on being with me, which made my stomach churn at the possibility she would try to harm Cosette. I also needed to do some digging to find out what Rosie was up to, what she was looking for in the library. *When had she become so secretive and hardened?*

Whatever had happened to her in the past 150 years had changed her. Desperate people did desperate things. Finding the true depth of Rosie's desperation wasn't going to be easy. She was no longer the same woman I knew, the one whose emotions I used to be able to read with such ease.

On my walk home, I contemplated how I could sniff out Rosie's true motives for appearing after nearly a century and a half and to how remove her from my life for good. My deep, strong feelings for Cosette surprised me. I couldn't believe I had turned away Rosie. I would have done anything to have Rosie back in my life many years ago. But when presented with a choice between the two, I wanted Cosette, with every ounce within me.

Crossing the threshold into my flat, I couldn't wait to have a soothing glass of blood. It had been one hell of a day, and I was ready to relax and crawl into my bed for the night. Throwing on some gray sweatpants and a tattered old t-shirt, I climbed into bed. I fell asleep, wishing for nothing more than to have Cosette at my side.

***

Cosette's warm hands glided over my body. First over my clothing and then her hands snuck underneath my shirt and down my pants, grazing my cock. Her teasing always drove me crazy and tonight she had me wanting her more than ever. Ruby red lips left a trail of kisses down my neck, causing me to moan with pleasure. I toyed with her hair as the line of kisses continued down my chest and abdomen. Her hair tickled my nose and I inhaled her faint scent, a mixture of earth and wildflowers. The subtle fragrance enveloped me, calming me.

She planted her hand on my chest while she nibbled at the waistband of my sweatpants. I was tense with anticipation and excitement at the thought of what she had planned next. Gripping my pants she tugged the front down, allowing my length to spring forth, hard and erect. Her fingertips grazed my cock and ran up and down along its length before she gripped me in her hand. Stroking my shaft, I felt my length becoming harder before she flicked her tongue on the head of my cock.

I drew in a quick breath as her teeth scraped the underside of my length. She teased me by swirling her tongue around the head. Licking from the base to the tip sent shivers down my spine. Her mouth enveloped the length of me as she took me to the hilt. She hollowed out her cheeks and licked and sucked with unquenchable need.

"Oh gods, Cosette. That feels so damn good, *mon tresor*," I said.

Expecting her to continue, it shocked me when I heard a growl of a voice say, "She is *not* your treasure! I *am*!"

Surprise ripped through my body. I shot up in bed and opened my eyes to see Rosie hovering over my lap instead of Cosette.

"What the fuck are you doing here?" I yelled, pushing her off me.

"I thought my intentions were quite clear," she said with a smirk as she took a step toward me.

Putting my hands up and outstretching my arms, I took a step back. "Rosie, I told you I'm not interested. Dammit, I have moved on. Leave me and Cosette alone!"

"You thought I'd give up? Naive Alaric, would you have given up on the one thing you knew was meant to be yours?"

The vein in my forehead throbbed and my nostrils flared. She wasn't hearing me. Grabbing her around the upper arms, I gave her a shake to get her attention. Frustration continued to grow within me but I also couldn't shake the nagging feeling to try to let Rosie down gently. I wasn't sure if it was because of my previous feelings for her or my trepidation regarding what she could possibly do to Cosette and I.

I took in a large breath before saying, "Rosie, I am only going to say this once. I no longer desire to have you in my life. I do not love you and I do not need you. Leave and never come back. Do not speak to me or Cosette again. Go live your life. I wish you well," I said with firm authority.

She stared up at me holding her head high, satisfied she had riled me up. With a grin on her face, she snarled, "You'll regret this." And with that, she stormed out of my apartment, seemingly not the way she entered.

15

COSETTE

Present Day

A quiet night in was exactly what I needed. The past few days had been a blur of activity and taxing on my emotions. From my whirlwind relationship with Alaric to discovering he was a vampire, I needed a night to wrap my mind around everything and process. Nothing like a chick flick, a glass of wine, and cozy sweats to help me relax. I still felt uneasy in my apartment since the break-in but I was doing everything in my power to release my anxiety and enjoy myself.

The movie credits rolled as I dozed off on the couch. Bleary-eyed, I drug myself off the couch, dropping of my wine glass on the kitchen counter on the way to my bedroom. Skipping my nightly skincare routine, I climbed into bed, hoping to pass out in an alcohol-induced coma for the night.

Before fully succumbing to my drowsiness, I glanced at my phone. No new messages. Suddenly, I had the urge to text Alaric, to tell him goodnight. In the midst of typing my text, my vision blurred as the wine took effect. My phone slipped out of my hand and off the bed. I gazed at the phone on the floor, too tired to grab it. That was a problem for tomorrow's Cosette. Without giving the phone a second thought, I turned over in bed giving in to the haze.

Some time later, though I'm not sure how much time had passed, I'm jolted awake by a hand covering my mouth. Frozen with fear, I opened my eyes to see who was in the room with me, but it was too dark to make out any details. My nose and mouth were enveloped, making it difficult to breathe despite my shallow, rapid breaths. Clawing at the hand suffocating me was unsuccessful. I tried to scream but I felt dizzy and disoriented as sleep became harder to avoid. My limbs were heavy like bricks and I couldn't stop my eyes from closing, despite my panic. As if someone turned out the light, my vision went pitch black- as did my thoughts.

***

I snapped my eyes open and stark darkness surrounded me. My hands had been bound with rope and a gag was in my mouth. My joints ached and my head throbbed, somewhere in between a hangover and illness. I was hungry but if I had food, I would probably throw up. Not because of the wine, but because of my current situation and the most recent memories I could recall.

My neck hurt and my eyes struggled to adjust to the darkness of the room. The only source of light was from a tiny window at the top of the opposite wall. As I was examining my surroundings, I gazed down and wiggled my body, assessing myself for injuries. I was unharmed, just groggy. Realizing my necklace was missing, I slumped even further into the wall, flitting my eyes about the room as my hands rested in the space where the necklace used to be.

The room I was in appeared to be a cell-like structure in a basement. It was small, dank, and cold with stone walls that looked to be centuries old. The air was heavy with the smell of decay and old flour while the sound of any movements I made in the cell reverberated against the walls. I wrapped my arms around my knees, hoping to warm myself with just my thin pajamas on my back.

While this room resembled a jail cell, it didn't appear to be one. I was in a basement somewhere. Rising from my seated position, I walked around the room. Trying the wooden, dilapidated door, I was disappointed to find it locked. I wondered if this room was used for food storage centuries ago. *Who would own such a property? And why would they want anything to do with me?*

Returning to huddle in the corner, I rested my head on my knees. I heard footsteps approaching outside the door. Anticipation perked my perception as I lifted my head when I heard the door unlock and creak open, revealing a dark figure emerging from the shadows. My heart pounded in my chest and my hands trembled as I waited to see what would happen next.

"Hello, Cosette," said the figure. Surprise radiated throughout my thoughts and I sucked in a breath, realizing the figure knew my name.

"Hello? Who's there?" I said, though my words were too muffled by the gag to be heard.

"I don't believe we've been formally introduced." The shadow stepped into the moonlight streaming through the window, her footsteps sounding metallic and pointed, "I'm Rosie." She leaned down to lower my gag. Eye to eye with my captor, I realized she was quite pretty with eyes the color of the sea and golden rims around her irises. Her copper hair fell past her shoulders and into her face as sweeping ringlets.

Who was this woman? I shook my head, attempting to collect my thoughts. "Do I know you?" I stuttered getting the question out.

"No, but I know who you are, Cosette." A sly smile graced her face. My stomach dropped, bile burning at the back of my throat at the realization that my kidnapping hadn't been random.

I was so confused who this woman was and what she needed from me. "Why am I here? What do you want?"

"You have something of mine." She crossed her arms and jutted her chin out, her sage green eyes boring into me.

"What? What do I have? You can have whatever it is. Just let me go." I thrashed my arms against the bindings. I just wanted to go home.

She bent down until she was mere inches from my face before demanding, "Alaric. I want Alaric."

I tried to scoot away from her but I was up against the wall. I blinked slowly as I stared up at Rosie, at a momentary loss for words.

My eyes widened and I felt light-headed. "Alaric? What do you want with Alaric?"

"For a librarian, girl, you really are quite dumb. I want Alaric because he was mine *first.*"

I drew in a breath, the gag dangling around my neck.

"Are you telling me you're Alaric's Rosie? But how? I thought you were…"

Rosie let out a wicked laugh before baring her fangs to me. I choked on a breath with realization. *Dear God, this woman was THE Rosie and she was a vampire.*

"You mean Alaric turned you? He didn't kill you like he thought?" My thoughts raced as the pieces fell into place.

"Bingo. Maybe you're not as stupid as I thought. I shocked him by showing up unannounced. But, because of you, he was less than excited to see me."

Rosie turned her body away from me, stalking about the room.

"So, what do you want with me?"

She whipped around, rushing over so that her face was mere inches from mine. "I want you gone. Out of his life forever." Her voice was stern and threatening. She spoke to me with such hatred that it made it hard to reconcile the person in front of me with the person Alaric had described.

"What does Alaric want?" I asked timidly.

"Never mind what he wants. He doesn't know what's best for him." Rosie stepped back, anger radiating off of her.

"But I love him," I said with pure dedication.

"Ha! Love? He will never love you like he loves me. You're some stupid girl he stuck his dick in. You mean nothing to him," she said, vehemently.

Her words cut me to the core as tears streamed down my face.

Rosie laughed. "It's always *been* me and it will always *be* me. This isn't a fight you're going to win, little girl."

I didn't know what to say to her. I wouldn't win a fight against a 150-year-old vampire with my hands bound and my necklace gone. Even if I had my faculties and the necklace's protection, Rosie would eviscerate me before I could strike her. Alaric didn't know where I was, who I was with, or that I was in danger.

I still couldn't believe Rosie was here in front of me. She was supposed to be dead. I was pulled from my thoughts as she stalked around me, getting closer with each pass. She stopped in front of me. "Now, what am I going to do with you?"

I stared at her, unable to respond to her rhetorical question. *What was she going to do to me?*

Rosie leaned down to place the gag back in my mouth and left the room. I heard the lock engage and footsteps trailing away, leaving me in the cold, dark dungeon.

16

ALARIC

Present Day

The next morning, as per my usual routine, I returned to the library to continue my research. Rosie's appearance had disrupted my plans for over a day, fueling my anxiety and leaving me distracted from her suspicious behavior. I felt uneasy knowing she was in town and didn't want to leave me alone. She was up to something.

Upon entering the library, I made a beeline to my usual study area in special collections. That morning, I found no useful new information which left me increasingly frustrated. At lunch, I emerged from the musty haven of ancient books, planning to ask Cosette to join me. I approached the desk to talk with her. Not seeing Cosette in her usual place behind the circulation desk in the lobby, I asked another librarian wearing a name tag reading, *Libby.* "Is Cosette available?"

She paused for a moment, biting her lower lip and tucking a strand of her blond bob behind her ear and said, "She isn't here today."

"She isn't?" I asked quizzically.

Reluctant to continue, she said, "She didn't show up to work today."

My eyes widened. "She didn't?"

"Yeah, I was going to check on her during my lunch break. I've tried calling her cell, but she hasn't answered." She shifted her weight from one foot to the other.

"Let me. I'll go to her apartment and check on her."

She eyed me with skepticism, sizing me up. I extended my hand to introduce myself.

"I'm sorry, I forgot to introduce myself. I'm Alaric, Cosette's boyfriend."

"Boyfriend?" She raised an eyebrow.

"I take it Cosette didn't mention me then?"

She shook her head.

"We met outside Club Dynamo. It's a new relationship, a bit of a whirlwind, actually. I do care for her quite a lot, though." I felt like a rambling, run-on sentence.

"Wait a minute," Libby said. "You're the guy she was so crazy for. She did mention you to me, I just didn't know your name."

I smiled with the realization that Cosette had discussed our relationship with one of her good friends. "I'll go check on her. There's probably a simple explanation for her absence."

"Thanks, Alaric. Hopefully she's just sick and there isn't something major going on. It's nice to meet you. Thank you for saving her that night. And for what it's worth, she really likes you too." She gave me a small smile.

"Of course, and nice to meet you as well."

With that, I left the library and hurried the short distance to Cosette's apartment. As I approached her door, I realized I didn't have a key to her place. If she didn't answer, I wasn't sure how to proceed. I knocked on the door, noticing the landlord had gotten around to fixing her door. With no answer, I knocked again, louder this time, calling out her name.

No answer.

Something was wrong. This wasn't like Cosette. I had no definitive proof, but I had a hunch that Rosie was involved. She had threatened me, saying I would be sorry for dismissing her. *Is this how she would make me sorry? Where would Rosie take her? Where was Cosette?*

17

COSETTE

Present Day

I had to pee, but there wasn't a bathroom in my medieval dungeon. Not even a bucket. *Someone must have noticed my absence from work by now. What was I supposed to do? What if no one came for me?* I was destined to feast upon the crumbs that were shared with the rats, and when those were gone, I was sure the rats would feast on me.

I hated feeling like a damsel in distress, but I couldn't do anything to change my current situation. Stone walls surrounded me on all sides with my only means of escape through a locked, wooden door or the small window, located high on a wall. I was not getting out of here unless I was dead or someone rescued me.

Suddenly, keys rattled and the door's lock clicked. "There's my little pet," Rosie said in a sing-song voice, after she unlocked the door and entered my cell.

With my head raised, I prayed she would show me mercy and allow me to leave. "What do you want, Rosie?" I asked, the gag muffling my question.

Yanking the gag from my mouth, she replied, "I wanted to see if you changed your mind."

"Rosie, I'm not leaving Alaric. There's nothing you can do to change my decision."

"Oh really? *Nothing* will change your mind? We'll see about that." She stalked around the room, her shoes making an audible click-clack on the stone floor.

Rosie smirked as she approached me. She grabbed a fistful of my hair and jerked my head backward so our eyes met. With me in her grip, she extended her arm backward, slapping my cheek. My head swiveled in the opposite direction. Another sharp blow stung my other cheek. I lowered my head and raised my bound hands to my face, shrinking away from her.

"You aren't as brave without *my* necklace, are you?" she asked. Her hands snuck under the neckline of her dress and revealed the ruby amulet hanging around her neck.

"Your necklace?" I wrinkled my eyebrows, feigning confusion.

"I was the one who gave Alaric that necklace, you stupid, little girl. It was for his protection, not yours. Imagine my surprise when you showed up with my necklace around your neck," she fumed.

Silent tears streamed down my face while I crouched in the corner, desperate to escape Rosie. She glared at me, rage sweeping across her face, thwarted in getting what she wanted. She began pacing, appearing to contemplate her next move. Frustrated, she clenched her fists and growled under her breath. Rosie turned and stormed out, slamming the wooden door shut. Her footsteps echoed on the stone floor and disappeared down the hallway.

Alone again in my cell, I wrapped my arms around myself for warmth, realizing I was going to have to pick a corner to designate as my bathroom. I choked at the thought of rooming with my excrement. Meanwhile, my stomach growled and my mouth felt dry from dehydration. With each passing hour, I felt weaker and weaker. If no one came for me, this dank room would be the place of my ultimate demise.

18

ALARIC

Present Day

I had to find her. I knew Rosie had her somewhere in McCallum. She did this to get to me, so she wouldn't take Cosette far. She *wanted* me to find her. Think Alaric, think. *Where would she take her?* I wasn't familiar with this new Rosie or her motivations. My mind raced with possibilities. Maybe she took Cosette somewhere in the original settlement.

Like a typical New England historic settlement, McCallum had plenty of important buildings dating back to the 19th century. These buildings were no longer used daily and could serve as the perfect venue. Rosie would need to keep Cosette hidden and somewhere where she had privacy.

After not finding Cosette in her apartment, I headed back to my place to formulate a plan to track down Cosette. I opened my laptop and did a quick internet search for the *McCallum Massachusetts Historical Society* website. It listed all buildings within the city that were designated as historical landmarks. Scrolling through the listings, I filtered the results based on the year built.

At the top of the filtered list was a listing for a factory, the *Bath Brothers Grain Factory*, built circa 1870. Bingo. The building was in the city's original manufacturing district, a part of town I had frequented since landing in McCallum in 1873. That part of town was mostly well-preserved yet unused, leaving ample opportunity to hide someone.

From the online description, the building was constructed of stone and wood with a basement for storing grain. The factory appeared small and wasn't currently being used as far as I could tell. A feeling in the pit of my stomach told me this is where I would find Cosette, but I needed to do some reconnaissance first.

I closed my laptop and began gathering my supplies to stake out the factory. I grabbed my backpack and put in some jars of blood, in case my cravings overwhelmed me. Then I added my camera with a telescopic lens, my cell phone, binoculars, and a book. I planned to stay nearby for a while, hoping to spot Rosie accessing the building. With one last check of my supplies, I grabbed my backpack and headed out.

As my apartment was close to the main part of town, it didn't take long for me to walk to the manufacturing district. Once the factory was in sight, I slowed my approach, scanning the area for any recognizable faces and securing a vantage point for my stakeout. As I studied the buildings surrounding the factory, I realized that I had limited options for observation. Across the street was an old textile mill, but the building next to the grain factory offered better surveillance and access.

I hid out in what used to be a flour mill. The buildings were close enough together that I could jump from roof to roof if needed. Hopefully, I could access the building through the roof. I needed to find Cosette before it was too late. Without food or water, she couldn't last more than a few days. Gods knew what Rosie planned to do with her either.

I sucked in a breath. I had to hang tight, watch the building, and devise a plan. I camped out on the top floor of the mill among the flour residue and the dust. Using my binoculars, I observed the building. No activity. No people. I was in for a long night. Settling into my corner for the evening, I attempted to make my presence as inconspicuous as possible by curling myself up on the floor below the windows.

Hours later, it was the middle of the night, and my stakeout continued. The mill was quiet enough to hear a pin drop, my breathing providing the soundtrack for the evening. A scratching noise caught my attention, my body stiffening to the alert. But I didn't notice the figure behind me before it was too late. A hand clamped over my mouth and another arm hooked my arms behind my back. I struggled, trying to free myself from my attacker's grasp, but I was overpowered. Darkness enveloped me when a flour sack was placed over my head.

I stumbled over my feet as I was led down the stairs. My attacker didn't speak, leaving me to guess what was in store for me. Soon, my footsteps changed from the mill's echo to the concrete street. My footsteps then turned to a dull sound with each stride and I felt the smoothness of the stone underfoot. Whether I had intended it or not, I had earned myself admission to the grain factory.

As I suspected, I was led down some steps. The footsteps of my captor and I along the stone floor echoed in my ears. I'm guided to turn and shoved into a seated position, before the flour sack was ripped off my head. My vision adjusted to the darker surroundings while I tried to confirm where I was. The opaque outline of the doorway came into focus.

"Hello, Alaric," the figure said from the doorway.

"Rosie." I clenched my jaw and my knuckles went white as I fisted my hands.

"What do I owe the pleasure of your presence tonight?" She stalked into the cell.

"You know why I'm here. Where's Cosette?" I asked through gritted teeth, struggling to stand.

"I'm not sure what you mean." She grinned coyly.

"Yes, you do! I know you have her. Now let her go!" I growled, reaching a standing position.

Rosie gave me a cunning look. She was clearly enjoying my distress. "Rosie, please. I beg of you. Let me see Cosette."

"What's in it for me?"

"What is it you want?" I asked, already knowing.

"You. I want you. I want us to be together again."

I took a step back. "I can't. Rosie, I've already told you. I love Cosette and I never want to be without her. You and I are never going to happen."

Enraged, Rosie stepped toward me and slapped me across the face. "You're a fool Alaric. You just signed both your death warrants." I attempted to lunge toward her but was restrained by my captor's hands.

She stormed out of the room, leaving me confined while her associate, my assumed attacker, tied my hands behind my back. Rosie's wingman was all muscle and easily tipped the scales at close to 300 pounds. He had to be around six foot tall with greasy blond hair and dark, pissed-off eyes.

A few minutes later, Rosie emerged with another dark figure from the hallway. Cosette stepped into the light streaming from the window with a grain sack over her head.

Rosie shoved her to the opposite wall and pulled the sack from her head.

"Here's your precious treasure," she said with saccharine in her voice.

"Alaric?" Cosette said, her eyes wide.

"I'm here, *mon tresor.*" I wanted to run to her, hug her, and tell her everything was going to be okay.

Rosie rolled her eyes and made gagging sounds in the background.

"How did you find me?" Cosette cried out. She tried to approach me, but Rosie held up her arm to block her.

"I told you I would always protect you. I'll always find you. No matter where you are." I went to run to her but my attacker grabbed my arms, holding me back.

"Oh, please," Rosie chimed in.

Cosette seemed to be okay physically. I couldn't see any injuries, but I knew she had to be tired, hungry, and dehydrated. I needed to find a solution to get us out of here.

Rosie's minion released my roped arms before he moved to stand nearby in the room. He clearly served as the muscle for the operation, stalking around, watching the interaction between Cosette and I, waiting for instructions from Rosie.

Rosie gestured to her underling, saying, "Just as we discussed, Johnnie." She then turned and sauntered out of the room.

So the muscle had a name. Johnnie. Whatever he had up his sleeve wasn't good. Before I could react, Johnnie landed a punch straight to my right cheek. Bloody saliva flew out of my mouth and onto the floor. With my arms incapacitated, I attempted to use my shoulders to gain distance from him. Johnnie came for me again, snatching my hair in his grip and slamming me against the stone wall.

Cosette huddled in the corner, trembling with fear and crying. "Stop! Please!"

It killed me to watch her, unable to stop him. Keeping Johnnie's attention on me was my primary goal. As long as he was occupied with me he couldn't touch Cosette. If I had to, I could play this game all day.

Johnnie smacked me across the face, grabbed my hair, and kneed me in the groin, sending me to the floor in pain. As I cried out, Cosette stood up and approached Johnnie from behind. He was unaware of how close she was. In one quick swoop, she jumped and swung her tied hands over Johnnie's head and around his neck, choking him. Johnnie bucked and rolled her off his back. He slung her into the wall like a rag doll, leaving her stunned.

Johnnie stormed out of the room and slammed the door shut, locking it. "Cosette," I said, attempting to meet her gaze, "are you okay? I'm here. I'll get us out of this, I swear." Before she could respond, Johnnie returned with a chair and some rope.

"Have a seat," he said, gruffly.

"Fuck, no." I said, staring daggers into his eyes.

"I *said*, have a seat." He forced me into the chair and tied my legs together, then looped the rope around to secure me tightly to the chair.

"Now, let's see what you do when I have my way with your little girlfriend here."

He turned, focusing his attention on Cosette. "What should I do with you, little princess?"

I watched as Cosette swallowed and steeled herself for what was about to happen, her eyes glued on him as she sat on the floor. My stomach churned with anxiety and my chest began to ache with anticipation. I knew we were at the breaking point and all hell was about to break loose. I continued to struggle against the rope holding me captive, desperately wanting to intervene between Johnnie and Cosette.

Johnnie grabbed her by the shirt, his face a mere inches from hers. "Open wide, little girl."

Silver lining her eyes, Cosette opened her mouth, allowing Johnnie to spit into it.

"Take it like the slut you are," Johnnie commanded.

Cosette looked him in the eyes and spit back his own phlegm into his face. "You fucking bitch!"

He slapped Cosette across the face and yanked her to the ground by her hair, slamming her head onto the stone floor. My body jerked in the chair as the rope held back my reflex to rescue her. Anger boiled within me as Cosette lay unconscious, blood seeping from her temple.

Johnnie continued to kick her before I yelled, "Stop! Get Rosie. I want to talk to Rosie *now!*"

He growled at me but stopped kicking Cosette and charged out of the room. After a short time, Rosie appeared.

"You requested my presence?" she asked, grinning demurely.

I looked at Cosette before I answered. She was moaning and had a slight shudder in her breathing. "I want you to let Cosette go-"

"And why would I do that?" Rosie interrupted, taking a step toward me.

"If you let Cosette go..." I paused when I saw Cosette's head roll to look at me through bleary eyes. "If you let her go, I'll stay with you."

I heard a tiny gasp. When I looked at Cosette, I could see tears rolling down her cheeks. The betrayal read broadly across her face.

"You'll stay with me? What do you mean?" Rosie said.

"Rosie, don't make me say it. I'll be with you if that's what you want."

"You'll give up your little treasure, just like that?" she asked, snapping her fingers for emphasis. "Forgive me, Alaric, if I don't fully believe you after all you've endured to rescue her."

"Believe me. Just let her go."

"Prove your seriousness to both of us. Then, I'll let her go...eventually." She paused for a moment looking from me to Cosette. "Kiss me," she said.

I shifted uncomfortably in my chair as she approached me. She bent down until she was level with my face and puckered her lips. Despite knowing this was going to crush Cosette, I gave her a quick apologetic look before I kissed Rosie with as much gusto as I could muster.

19

COSETTE

Present Day

In a single moment, my heart shattered into a thousand pieces. Right in front of my eyes, Alaric kissed Rosie with the same passion I'd seen him have for me. Their tongues intertwined, making me equally devastated, enraged, and shocked. What was only a few seconds felt like a lifetime as I watched.

A flashback to our first kiss on the bridge erupted in my thoughts. Memories of the feel of his touch and embrace, the physical and emotional reactions he elicited in me poured into my consciousness. Remembering the way his kiss made my stomach flip and my toes curl brought me to my figurative knees.

How could he do this to me? He so easily gave up fighting Johnnie and agreed to be with Rosie.

Rosie pulled back, releasing Alaric from the kiss. She looked over her shoulder and smiled at me with a Cheshire grin. She seemed to enjoy this and reveled in my heartache, making the situation worse.

Rosie licked her lips. "Mmm, you taste just like I remember, Alaric."

Alaric said nothing as he stared blankly ahead. I shut my eyes as they filled with tears, and a sharp pain radiated through my chest. I heard her footsteps leave the room, but upon opening my eyes, I realized she had returned quickly with another chair and additional rope.

Rosie placed the seat opposite Alaric, facing him. She gripped my upper arm to move me to a standing position, then guided me to sit. She shoved me down, and while she tied my arms and legs with rope to the chair, I stared into Alaric's eyes.

"Now, my dear, we'll see how dedicated your little love is to being with me. Let's see if he really can leave your simple self behind." Rosie purred at me with a sickly smile.

Alaric and I both sat in silence, our eyes torn between making eye contact and avoiding looking at each other. When I did meet his gaze, I felt as if he was trying to convey something to me with his eyes, something he couldn't say out loud.

Rosie approached Alaric, positioning her body between us. She cupped his face. "Let's continue, my love. I'm going to untie your hands, but if you try anything, I'll kill her."

Without a word, Alaric swallowed and nodded.

Rosie, taking her time, undid the ropes securing Alaric's hands. Still secured to the chair, he didn't move. I sat watching Rosie as she walked around Alaric, caressing him with her hands. I was being forced to watch a seduction in real time.

ALARIC

Present Day

My hands were free, but I had to be careful. I couldn't try to overpower Rosie or she'd kill Cosette. If I tried to talk to Cosette or even look at her, I worried that wouldn't go over well either. Still tied to the chair, I wouldn't be able to untangle myself in enough time to rescue her if she was attacked. Rosie's hands ran over my skin in sweeping strokes as gooseflesh erupted over my body. The sensations caused my body to betray me despite the unwanted touches. It disgusted me to have these feelings coming from her actions.

Upping the ante, Rosie straddled my thighs and kissed me. When I didn't react, she pulled back to give me a look that told me my participation was necessary. I kissed her in return. Pulling back to end the kiss, she looked me suspiciously in the eye before she trailed kisses down my neck. Nature betrayed me as my dick became hard and throbbed against my pants as she rocked and ground her hips in my lap.

Rosie smirked, enjoying how I responded physically to her. Her hands skirted the hem of my shirt before she pulled it over my head, leaving my chest bare. She then ran them down my chest and over my pants. She turned herself around, so she was sitting on my lap, facing Cosette. I couldn't see Rosie's face, though I surmised she was doing so to throw this in Cosette's face.

Cosette's face was splotchy and reddened, evidence of her silent sobbing. My fists clenched as I fought the need to comfort her. Rosie continued her lap dance before turning to face me again. This time she looked at me with a devilish grin, and I realized the situation was about to get worse.

With my eyes closed, I tried to calm myself down, imagining the saddest thoughts I could muster, willing my dick to shrink. Rosie's hands were on my waistband, fumbling with the button. She popped my pants open, pulled down my boxers, and allowed my cock to spring forth.

"Well, well, well, what do we have here?" Rosie chided. She glanced over a shoulder to Cosette, smiling and with a malicious gleam in her eyes. Cosette's eyes grew dull and tears welled in them"I know. He is quite a prize. I can see why you would want him. Just remember, I had him first, and I'll have him last."

Rosie laughed maniacally while stroking my cock. I didn't want to like it and I didn't want to enjoy it. I wanted to be doing this with Cosette, not this fucked up lap dance routine with Rosie. She stroked me from root to tip. My cock pulsed as Rosie gripped me harder and increased the speed of her caress.

My breath quickened. "Someone likes their dick stroked. Let's see what you think about this."

While Cosette watched in horror, Rosie kneeled on the floor and dipped her head, taking my cock in her mouth. She began sucking the tip before taking me further into her mouth. As she bobbed up and down the length of my dick, her teeth gently scraped the underside of my shaft and, as she approached the tip, she swirled her tongue around the head.

I was going to come and there was nothing I could do to prevent myself from reaching orgasm. Rosie was going to make me come in front of Cosette. The pressure of my orgasm approached, my body trembling as I tried to prevent it from happening.

Rosie noticed my reaction and withdrew her mouth. "We can't have that happening yet. Not until I've had your cock buried in me. You need to prove yourself to me, Alaric."

"I can't do that tied to this chair, Rosie," I said flatly.

"Don't worry about that. I'll take care of you, my dear."

She smashed her mouth to mine. In another life, the kiss would have been hot, but all that registered was the sloppiness and how much I detested Rosie. Rosie hiked up her dress, positioned herself over my lap, and plunged downward onto my erection. My body betrayed me further, as the sensation felt glorious. I didn't want it to feel this good, but as Rosie continued to rock her body on my lap, my arousal continued to heighten. Her motions became quicker while she rode me and rubbed her clit.

"Come with me, Alaric."

Her statement was a command and I wouldn't be able to hold back my orgasm much longer. I pulled every disgusting or sad thought I could think of in my brain, attempting to avoid the inevitable. From thoughts of cold showers and ex-girlfriends, I was unable to prevent the pressure building deep within me. While biology was the ultimate betrayer, my feelings were true and meant for Cosette. As I reached the crest of my climax, I called out, "Oh gods!"

"That's my Alaric. You like how that feels, don't you? I bet your little treasure can't make it feel this good."

Rosie continued her ministrations until she crested through her own orgasm. She rested her head on my chest while my regretful eyes bore into Cosette's. I tried to convey what was going on in my mind to her, but she glanced away. Rosie removed herself from my lap, letting her skirt fall to the floor while leaving my flaccid cock exposed as proof of my infidelity. She quickly retied my bindings, preventing me from using my hands.

The sorrow I experienced during and increasingly afterward stared me in the face before I hung my head and gazed at my lap. I was in an impossible situation that I wasn't sure either Cosette or I could escape.

I raised my head to meet Rosie's eyes. "I did what you asked. Now let Cosette go." I said through gritted teeth.

"Are you really that naive, Alaric?" Rosie raised one eyebrow as she studied me.

I glared at her. Frustration boiled within me and I was about to become a desperate man. "I am a man of my word, Rosie, and I expect you to follow through with our agreement. If you won't, then I cannot be with you," I growled as I jerked in my chair.

"You're not in a position to be changing your mind or ordering me around, are you?"

"Please, I'm begging you, let her go." I pleaded, my voice cracking.

Rosie huffed and rolled her eyes. "Fine."

She walked behind Cosette's chair and began untying her. As the ropes fell away, Cosette whipped her body around, swinging her arms violently in an attempt to strike Rosie. Rosie gripped Cosette's wrists together in one hand while grabbing her hair with the other.

"You little bitch," she sneered. Rosie used her strength to leverage Cosette's neck to the side while displaying her fangs. "I let you go, and this is how you repay me? This ends *now!*"

With that, Rosie plunged her fangs into Cosette's neck. Cosette cried out from the pain, blood running down her neck as Rosie fed from her.

20

ALARIC

Present Day

The rope that bound my hands flexed tautly as I struggled to be released from their grip. In front of my eyes, Rosie drained Cosette while I watched as the life slipped from her body. Using all my strength, I wriggled and fiddled with my bindings until the rope offered some slack and I released myself from the chair.

With my newfound freedom, I quickly tucked my dick back into my pants and raced over, grabbing Rosie by the shoulders and pulling her away from Cosette.

"Get off of her!" I yelled, slamming Rosie into the stone wall. Rosie and I dueled against each other, Rosie matching each of my strikes with her own. Our punches, slaps, and yanking grew sloppier by the second as we tired.

With her last bit of strength, Rosie pushed me into the wooden chairs, which shattered into a million pieces.

Shock coursed through me. I never thought Rosie would hurt me. or be aggressive towards me. I didn't know this Rosie in front of me and it saddened me to see the difference. Reflecting back to our time together many years ago, I remembered Rosie fondly, her laugh when I would make an inappropriate comment or when something was extremely funny. The difference was so stark it gutted me.

As I tried to collect myself into an upright position, Rosie turned her attention back to Cosette and kicked at her slumped body. Adrenaline shot through me, allowing me to hyperfocus on the situation at hand. Feeling a piece of broken wood underneath my hand, I gripped the wood before flinging myself toward Rosie.

I pinned her to the floor, straddling my legs over her hips, and I used my weight to prevent her from moving. Rosie fought and squirmed beneath me with every ounce of spirit she had left. I gathered her wrists in my hands and pinned them on either side of her head.

"Please don't, Alaric," she pleaded as she writhed under my grip.

"Rosie, it has to be done. You've damaged everything you've come into contact with. You have tried to kill my relationship with Cosette and eliminated anything in your path that you didn't like. I can't let you continue to destroy lives." My voice grew raspy with anticipation as I knew what I was about to do. "You have turned into someone I don't know. We have no chance of being together. I no longer love you. I love Cosette and want to spend my life with her. You need to be gone and the only way I can ensure you will never bother her or us again is by eliminating you. For good." My hands shook and my muscles tightened with readiness as I battled my sadness over the way things had turned out.

"No, no, no, no! Please! I'll leave and never bother you again. I swear! Alaric, don't!" Rosie thrashed against my grip in an attempt to grab the makeshift stake out of my hands.

I held the splintered piece of wood over my head and poised to sink it into her chest. "I'm sorry it had to end this way. Goodbye, Rosie."

With my last farewell, I plunged the wooden spike deep within her chest. Blood oozed from her as the life drained out of her eyes. In a full circle moment, her body looked as it did when I drained her over a century ago and I felt a rush of sadness at the reminder.

Bringing my thoughts to the present, I crawled over to where Cosette lay. She was slumped on the floor in a lifeless heap. I gathered her into my arms, whispering to her.

"I've got you, *mon tresor*. She won't bother us anymore," I said, stroking her hair. She was breathing but unconscious, with bruises and dried blood covering various places along her body.

I checked her pulse and breathing, noticing both were slower than I'd like. Assuming she had lost too much blood, I deployed my fangs and pierced the inside of my wrist. Blood dripped from my arm as I held it up to Cosette's mouth.

"Come on, babe. I need you to drink from me. You've lost too much blood. This will help you feel better."

No response.

"Cosette, please. Work with me." The blood continued to flow in her mouth and dripped out the side of her lips

"*Mon tresor.* I need you to swallow, Cosette." With my fingers, I lightly pressed on her chin to close her mouth, willing her to swallow.

Her eyes fluttered, and she roused slightly.

"Drink, baby, please," I pleaded. "You need to drink some more." Cosette groaned, still out of it. With her eyes closed, she placed her hands around my wrist and drank.

"That's my girl," I praised. She took a few more gulps, which perked her up. "How are you feeling?" I asked.

"Like shit." She let out a small chuckle and I grinned in response.

"That's to be expected, I suppose."

Looking around, she said, "What happened?" Her eyes landed on Rosie's body, blood oozing from her chest.

"It's over, *mon tresor*. We don't have to worry about Rosie any longer. She's dead, for good."

"I don't understand. I don't get it," she said.

Amused, I let out a laugh. "What do you mean? Cosette, I could never let her hurt you any more than she already did. I would never have let her hurt you if I could have intervened."

"What happened to your desire to be with Rosie? You let her give you a blow job…in front of me. You had *sex* with her…*in front of me!*"

"Cosette, I didn't want those things from her. I wanted them from you. I had to play along with her little game so she wouldn't hurt you further. You were the reason I got through it all. Seeing you, as hard as it was, was the only way I could stay the course. Everything I did, I did for you. You're who I want, Cosette. I love you. All of that was part of my plan to keep you safe. I didn't want it to go that far, but I worried that if I didn't comply, she'd kill you."

Cosette stared at me with an expression that begged me to continue.

"When I killed Rosie the first time, I grieved for her. I thought she was the love of my life. But I was wrong. So, so wrong, Cosette. *You* are the love of my life. I didn't realize

185

there was an emptiness in me until you filled it. You're all I think about. Your love has made me a better person, and I can't imagine life without you. *You* are my treasure, and I'll never let you go."

Tears welled up in Cosette's eyes. She embraced me and delivered a kiss straight from her heart to mine. I deepened the kiss, and she returned in kind. I pulled away from the kiss and searched her eyes for meaning.

"*Mon tresor*, will you have me? Can you forgive me for all those awful things you had to endure?"

She thought for a long moment, causing me to hold my breath. When she finally responded, she said, "Yes. I can forgive you." With a smile that reached my eyes, I gathered her in my arms and swung her around, elated with joy. I lowered her down and glanced around the room. "You ready to get out of here?"

"Yes," she whimpered. "What about the body? And Johnnie?"

"If you can wait a few more minutes, I'll take care of it and make sure he's gone," I said.

"I'll just sit right here," she said weakly.

I gave her a quick kiss on the cheek and stepped out of the cell to see if I could find Johnnie. Not wanting to get too far from Cosette, I looked up and down the darkened hallway. There was no sign of Johnnie or anyone else. The mill appeared to be empty.

With the coast clear, I went about disposing of Rosie's body. The only place I could use was the nearby river. The mill was located on McCallum's waterway and would serve as Rosie's final resting place.

I found several large industrial flour sacks, using them to encase her body. Using some rocks from the shoreline, I stuffed the sacks to weigh her body down. For added measure, I wrapped some rope I found in the mill around the sacks, adding more rocks.

I bowed my head and closed my eyes in reverence before saying, "I'm sorry it had to be this way, Rosie. I'm sorry it didn't work out for us. I hope that you will forgive me for what I did, I know you would have done the same to protect me."

With a final sigh, I launched her body into the water, watching her sink and the current sweep her out further into the river. I stood at the water's edge for another minute, reflecting on what had transpired in the previous hours. Once I was satisfied Rosie wouldn't be washing ashore, I headed inside to check on Cosette.

As I entered the cell once again, Cosette sat on the ground with her knees to her chest and her head on her knees. "You ready to go, *mon tresor?*"

"Yes," she whispered.

She was still incredibly weak from blood loss, so I scooped her up in my arms, saying, "Let's get you home."

21

COSETTE

Present Day

S afe in Alaric's arms, I buried my face in the curve of his neck, encircling it with my arms, and drawing him close. Alaric walked us out of the basement and up the stone steps to the street level. In no hurry, we made our way in silence down the street and into Alaric's neighborhood.

Outside his apartment door, he looked down at me and whispered, "Is this okay?"

"Yes."

"I figured you would feel safer here, but I can always take you back to your place," he said, opening the door and crossing into the threshold.

"No, I want to stay here. With you." I leaned up and kissed his neck. Then, he bent down and kissed my forehead.

"Good. I couldn't stand to be away from you right now."

"Me, either." I gave him a small smile as he carried me to his bedroom and sat me on the bed.

He stood back, examining me. "We should get you into some new clothes."

I looked down at my bloodied and torn pajamas, soiled from the events of the past twenty-four hours. "Yeah, you're right."

Rustling around in his chest of drawers, Alaric pulled out a pair of sweatpants, a t-shirt, and a hoodie. "Here, let me help you," he said, lifting the hem of my shirt over my head.

I winced as I lifted my arms above my shoulders. He slipped his t-shirt and hoodie onto me. The hoodie's large size enveloped me in softness and warmth. Assisting me to stand, he removed my pants and offered his shoulders to steady me as I pulled on the sweatpants. His scent mixed with laundry detergent still lingered on the fabric, calming me.

"Can I get you anything? Some food? A drink?"

I shook my head and held my stomach as it churned with nausea. "No. I'm okay. I don't think I could eat a thing. I'm just tired."

"You want to get some sleep?"

"Will you just hold me for now?"

"You don't even have to ask."

We crawled under the covers with Alaric spooning me. He placed his arm around my middle and drew me closer to him. I felt and heard him sniffing my hair as he left a trail of kisses on my neck.

"I love you," he whispered in my ear.

"I love you too."

"I'll always protect you, Cosette, no matter what it takes to keep you safe. I'd do anything for you."

I turned over in bed so that we were face to face. "You already have."

"And I'd do it all over again. I love you so much, *mon tresor*," he said, giving me a squeeze and holding me close.

"I love you too."

"Ready for bed?"

"Yes, after the last couple of days, rest is exactly what I need."

Alaric reached up to turn off his bedside lamp, enveloping us in soothing darkness.

***

I stayed at Alaric's for the next two days, resting and relishing in the safety and comfort of his apartment. Waking up in Alaric's bed, I rolled over, snuggling into his side. "Good morning," I croaked, kissing him.

Despite how sore and bruised I was, I had a burning desire to be as close to him as possible. My hands roamed over his body landing on his muscled chest. He ran his hands down my body while looking at me with his crystal blue eyes. His eyes met mine, silently asking if he could continue.

My hands slid down his chiseled abs, slipping below the waistband of his sweats. His cock was already rock hard, leaving me wanting him inside of me as soon as possible. Caressing the length of him, I hoped to communicate what we were doing was okay. I wanted him just as much.

As I stroked faster and with increased pressure, Alaric fisted my hair while deepening our kiss. I gripped him harder, communicating my aching need to have him do the most naughty and inconceivable things to me. He groaned in pleasure, succumbing to my actions.

Alaric's hands traveled down my body and into the sweatpants I had borrowed from him. When he reached my apex, I let out a tiny squeal and shuddered with anticipation. He began stroking my pussy with soft and gentle touches as I moaned into his mouth. His fingers grazed up and down the length of my slit.

We sat in bed, letting our hands explore the other's body. The stroking, touching, and panting were reaching a fever pitch. He withdrew his fingers from me, my pussy aching from his absence, and examined the glistening arousal before smoothing his finger across my upper lip and then placing them in his mouth.

As he licked my juices, I continued with fervent strokes until he said, "I hope you know what you're doing."

Licking my upper lip, I giggled before putting my mouth on his. "What do you mean?" I said, pulling back from our kiss.

"Because after everything, I want nothing more than to have you. *All* of you."

"I'm not sure what you mean," I said while coyly biting my lower lip.

"I want all of you. Every inch. Every hole. You are mine, and I want to show every part of you how much I love you."

I swallowed as he continued.

"Don't worry. We'll take it slow. I would never hurt you. I only want you to feel pleasure from the things we do together."

"I trust you, Alaric."

He kissed me passionately, and I knew our sexual relationship was about to progress farther than we had ever gone before. I did trust him. There was nothing we could do together that could scare me. Despite my nerves around new sexual experiences, Alaric was the perfect person to experience it with.

I felt safe with him and knew he would be gentle with me. Yet I somehow knew he would deliver on my greatest fantasies. The pleasure I knew I would glean from this made my heart beat with excitement and anticipation.

"You are mine, Cosette. Never forget that." He growled in my ear.

"As long as you keep reminding me," I grinned.

"Don't worry, I will." He smiled, continuing, "Touch me, Cosette. I want to feel how much you want this, how badly you want me."

I rolled our bodies, so Alaric was now on top of me. I had access to his pulsating cock, and I loved the dominant feel of him hovering above me. Still clad in our clothes, I circled my legs around his waist, drawing him closer to me.

Through kisses, we rocked our bodies together, feeling each other over and then under our clothing. As Alaric gazed down over me, he slid his body down mine, leaving a trail of kisses alternating with sensual groans. He peeled my sweatpants from my body.

Spreading my thighs wider, he licked his lips, murmuring, "Beautiful." He lowered his face to my apex, delivering delicate licks and sucks. "You taste so sweet and delectable. I can't get enough of you, Cosette."

"Alaric," I breathed.

"Tell me what you want, baby," Alaric said, seductively.

"Everything."

"Your wish is my command."

With renewed determination, Alaric feasted on me like a man starved. He flooded me with pleasure in multiple places. While his mouth concentrated on my swollen nub, his fingers curved inside of me, bringing me closer to orgasm. I felt his finger linger at my asshole, causing me to tense slightly at the new sensation. Taking his time, Alaric inserted his pinky finger into my ass. The added pressure and pleasure sent me over the edge, careening into back-to-back orgasms.

"That's my girl," he praised. "You like that, *mon tresor?*"

"Yes. Don't stop," I whimpered.

"I've got a better idea." Hungry for more, Alaric flipped me over, positioning me on all fours.

"Exquisite," he murmured. He trailed his fingers from my hair down my spine, in between my butt cheeks and ending at my slit. Kissing each butt cheek, he murmured, "Wait one moment."

I was giddy with anticipation while I heard Alaric rummaging around the room behind me.

"I want to make sure you're ready for me. Let's get you all prepared."

Hearing the sound of a squeeze bottle, I looked over my shoulder to see him slathering lube on his index finger. He swirled his finger around my rear opening.

"Relax, *mon tresor.* I've got you," he said, while laying a reassuring hand on my hip.

I gasped as he slowly advanced his finger forward into my ass. Even with one finger, I felt full and incredibly turned on. I had no idea how I was going to accommodate his dick when his finger already had me feeling so stretched.

"Look how well you open up for me, Cosette. You like this, don't you?"

"Uh huh. It feels amazing."

Alaric continued to work my ass by adding a second finger. His fingers slipped in and out of me with ease. With his other hand, he reached around to stroke my clit. The pleasure from opposite ends was equally distracting and each movement made it feel as if sparks were coursing through me. It was almost impossible for me to focus on one particular sensation of pleasure while feeling as full as possible. As I was reaching the precipice of another orgasm, Alaric withdrew his fingers.

I whimpered at the loss of his penetration.

"Don't worry, my love, you won't be empty for long."

Nervous with anticipation, I gazed behind me to see him stroking his glorious length while slathering on more lube. Primed and lingering at the entrance to my ass, he hesitated for a moment.

"Take a deep breath, Cosette," Alaric said with gentle reassurance.

I breathed deeply and exhaled as Alaric slid the tip of his dick in, slowly stretching me. Mewling with pleasure, he withdrew and then advanced inch by inch, praising me the entire way.

"You feel amazing. Look at how we fit together. Gods, it feels like you were made for me. I love you, Cosette," Alaric confessed as he stilled inside me.

"I love you too, Alaric. You feel so good."

He continued to inch his way inside until he was buried in me. Pausing for a moment, Alaric demanded,

"Touch yourself, Cosette. I want to watch you play with your clit while I'm buried deep inside you."

"Yes, sir," I joked.

Alaric moaned. "Be careful, *mon tresor*. It makes me feral when you say that."

I continued to rub my clit while Alaric pumped into my ass. "I'm close, Alaric."

"Oh, Cosette, I'm going to come. Come for me, baby. Tell me you're mine."

"I'm yours." I struggled to get the words out. Not because I didn't believe it, but because I was about to tumble over the cliff into ecstasy.

"And you." *Thrust.* "Are." *Thrust.* "Mine." *Thrust.*

With a final thrust, Alaric filled me to the brim before collapsing on top of me. After a few silent moments, he raised his head and used his fingers to direct my gaze over my shoulder before he planted a smoldering kiss on my lips.

Unfurling ourselves from each other, Alaric grabbed a towel from the nearby bathroom and began cleaning me up. His tender touch traveled to every crevice, wiping up the results of our lovemaking. Thoroughly satisfied with his work, he chucked the towel into the hamper

"That was amazing, Cosette. How do you feel? Are you okay?" he said, gathering me in his arms.

Smiling, I said, "I'm great. It went beyond any expectations I had."

"In a good way?"

"Yes! In a good way."

He kissed me again. "Care to join me in the shower?"

"Only if I get the shower head the majority of the time." I laughed.

"You'll have to beat me to it!" Alaric took off running toward the bathroom.

I took off running after him, laughing the entire way. I slammed into his naked backside in the bathroom before we collapsed into a heap of laughter on the floor.

Tucking a strand of hair behind my ear, Alaric said, "I sure do love you Cosette, from now until eternity." Then, he placed a kiss squarely on my lips.

"I love you too, Alaric," I continued with the largest grin on my face, "to the moon and back."

EPILOGUE

ALARIC

Present Day | Six Months Later

"You got it?" Cosette asked.

"I got it, *mon tresor*. Don't worry," I said in between grunts as I supported a giant box on my chest. Cosette flitted around me, bracing for me to drop the box.

"They're just really old and valuable." She cringed as I juggled the box of her precious books.

I chuckled at her worry. "I know, baby, but I promise I got it. I'm not going to let anything happen to your cherished first editions."

"Here, let me get the door," she said, scrambling to open the entrance to my apartment.

"Thanks." I passed by her and walked into the living room, placing the box delicately on the floor. "I have just the place for your books. Let me show you."

Grabbing her hand, I escorted her to the corner of the living room where a newly installed ornate bookcase sat.

201

"Alaric, it's beautiful." Cosette gazed at the intricate detailing, touching the swirls carved in the wood.

"I'm glad you like it." Her reaction made me smile from ear to ear.

"Where on Earth did you find a piece like this?" she asked.

Clearing my throat, I hesitated. "I made it."

"You *made* this?"

"I wanted you to have the perfect place for all your special books that you love so much."

Cosette rushed to me, flung her arms around my neck, and planted a kiss firmly on my mouth. "Thank you, I absolutely love it."

"I'm glad. Now let's go get the rest of your stuff."

I was ecstatic that Cosette was moving in with me. We had been together for six months and it just seemed right for us to live together. Our relationship had really grown since the whole ordeal with Rosie. The totality of the situation still weighed heavily on my mind, knowing the role I played in Rosie's death.

Everything I had learned about myself and Cosette in the process made me appreciate our relationship that much more. I cherished her and couldn't imagine my life without her. So much, in fact, that I had one last surprise up my sleeve.

"That's the last of it," Cosette said, dusting off her hands.

"You weren't kidding when you said you had a lot of stuff," I joked.

"Ha ha. At least I'm not 150 years old." Cosette stuck her tongue out at me.

"Technically, I'm 178 years old. But I'll always be perpetually 28 years old."

"Semantics," Cosette joked back.

I gathered her in my arms before saying, "At least I'll always be this good looking for you."

She swatted at me. "Hush."

Looking into her eyes, I squeezed her tighter. "I love you, *mon tresor.*"

"I love you too."

"Are you ready for your next surprise?" I asked.

"Another surprise?" She questioned me with a raised eyebrow.

"I guess you'll have to wait and see."

Less than an hour later, we were walking toward the waterfront. Memories of our first date flooded over me. When I caught sight of the bridge where we had our first kiss, nostalgia enveloped me, and I knew I had found the perfect spot.

With her hands in mine, I drew Cosette closer to me, gazing into her eyes. Slowly, I brought my lips down toward hers until a breath remained between us. I stared at her mouth, praying to the gods the next few minutes went smoothly. Our lips crashed together in a deep passionate embrace, our tongues dancing together in the deepened kiss. When we had untangled ourselves from each other, I began.

"Cosette, you are the light of life. You have brought so much brightness to my world. When I had accepted my life would be full of disappointment, grief, and hate, you showed up and changed everything for me. I don't know what I ever did to deserve you, but I am beyond thankful for you. You have taught me forgiveness, acceptance, and I never want to be without you," I confessed.

At this moment, I got down on one knee and opened a ring box displaying an antique diamond cluster ring. The gold band featured a marquise cut shape with seventeen smaller diamonds clustered within the arrangement.

I continued, removing the ring from the box. " Cosette, will you do me the honor of being my wife, for as long as you live?"

Cosette covered her face with her hands. Time stood still while I was down on one knee, waiting for Cosette's answer.

"Yes, yes. A thousand times, yes. Of course!" she exclaimed.

Before I could place the ring on her finger, she embraced me and I gathered her into a hug, swinging her around in a circle. I sat her down long enough to slide the ring on her finger.

Looking at her ring, Cosette said, "Wow. It's beautiful, Alaric. Where did you find this? Is it vintage?"

I smiled. "It is. It was my mother's."

I could see the thoughts swirling in her head. "And before you ask, no, I never gave this ring to Rosie."

Cosette's eyes widened. "Really? Why not?"

While she admired how the ring looked on her finger, I replied, "At the time, I didn't even think about it as an option. But now that I look back, I think it was because Rosie wasn't the right woman for the ring. You are. This was my mother's most treasured possession. And you, *mon tresor*, are my treasure."

With that, I tucked an errant strand of hair behind Cosette's ear, then cupped her face and kissed her. We continued our walk down the river before returning to our apartment to begin the rest of our lives.

ACKNOWLEDGEMENTS

First and foremost, thank you to my dear readers for accompanying me on this journey. It means the world to me that you took a chance on my debut novel. Thank you to my husband, who always supports me, no matter what hair-brained idea enters my mind. To my son, your creativity inspires me daily to dream up new and exciting stories to tell. I'm not sure I will ever match your imagination, but your inspiration is boundless. To Dad, I hope you never read this, but thank you for always supporting me, no matter what I wanted to do or be. Thank you for teaching me to love learning and that reading can take me far.

Shout out to all my fellow writers on Scribophile for your critiques, feedback, and support along the way. Thank you to Julie Schorr for your valued addition to the book cover design. Thank you to my Beta readers Amber Sanchez, D. Soledad, Sloan, and MacKenzie Runnalls. Thank you to author Amanda Nichole for your feedback and support to independent authors like myself. Special thanks to Sloan for additional assistance and editing of the manuscript and back cover content. I could not have completed this project without every single one of you. I hope you all will continue with me on my writing journey and join me for further publications.

All my love, L.T.

ABOUT THE AUTHOR

Born and raised in the Bluegrass state of Kentucky, L.T. Whitney lives with her loving husband, a son whose boundless curiosity fuels her imagination, and a menagerie of furry friends. You can find her buried in a book, crocheting, listening to true crime podcasts, or at her day job when she's not writing.

https://ltwhitneyauthor.substack.com

www.ltwhitneyauthor.com

Connect with her on social media @ltwhitneyauthor.

Be the first to know when L.T. Whitney's next book is available!

Follow her at https://www.bookbub.com/authors/l-t-whitney to get an alert whenever she has a new release, preorder, or discount!

www.ingramcontent.com/pod-product-compliance
Lightning Source LLC
Chambersburg PA
CBHW021032130626
46552CB00005B/1798